Kayla In Paris

A SERIOUSLY SPICY MISTAKEN IDENTITY ROMANTIC COMEDY

THEODORA TAYLOR

CHAPTER 1

Kayla

"Ooh, look who's a lucky passenger today!"

The first-class cabin's British flight attendant squeezed the top of the empty seat next to mine with a congratulatory wink. "I'd actually pay pounds to trade places with you right now, Ms. Edwards!"

No, you wouldn't. You so, so wouldn't. She had no idea why the seat beside mine was paid for but sitting empty. If she did, she'd probably pay pounds *not to be* me right now.

I glanced at the pretty gold band on her left hand. Heck, I would probably offer *her* money to trade places right now.

But it wasn't her fault I was flying alone to Paris on an all-expenses-paid luxury trip meant for two. No need to drag down her mood with the empty seat's sad backstory.

I opened my mouth to answer her congratulatory wink with a simple (and situation-appropriate) "thanks,"

But before I could get the word out, she waved a hand above her head and called down the aisle, "Right this way, Mr. Atwater! You're in seat 1B!"

Seat 1B.

Wait. That was the empty seat beside mine!

My heart lurched. I'd thought I was safe!

The seat next to me had remained empty on the first leg of my flight from Los Angeles to London's Heathrow Airport, thanks to Dwayne's unclaimed ticket, and the pilot had already made the takeoff announcement—in both French and English.

I figured Tourmaline Airlines must have a policy when it came to passengers who didn't show up for their first-class flights. I'd even fastened my seatbelt with the assumption that I'd be continuing the trip the way I'd started it. Alone.

But no....

Somebody was headed this way. To sit in the seat I'd so carefully chosen for Dwayne. Back when I thought I'd be flying to Paris as his girlfriend and coming back as his fiancée.

But now, the seat I chose for him groaned under the weight of some stranger.

Don't cry! Don't cry! I turned my face to the small window and squeezed my eyes shut. What was that British saying? *Stiff upper lip.*

Well, I clamped *both* of my lips, curling them under my teeth to keep the waterworks at bay. But it didn't work. Hot droplets of emotion broke free from my closed eyelids and spilled down my cheeks.

Those bitter tears cared not a fig that I was sitting in a luxurious first-class cabin next to a stranger who did not deserve to be stuck with a crying woman on their way to the City of Lights.... Or that Dwayne Thornhill wasn't worth a single one of my tears.

Hadn't I been humiliated enough by my NFL player ex?

He wasn't even that great of a football player—a second-string kicker known more for the showy dance he did on the rare occasion he made a field goal than his actual skills at playing the game.

He hadn't been that great of a boyfriend, either. Always broke because most of the money he made went to clothes, flashy cars, and going out to places where he'd be seen by the "right people."

I never did quite figure out who the right people were. Only who they weren't.

I wasn't the right people, which is why we could never just stay in and chill with Netflix. The right people also weren't my family, judging from the way he'd sigh and roll his eyes through my father's monthly cookouts. And the right people definitely weren't my boss and best friend, Suzie.

> *"Don't you think it's kind of weird that you spend so much time outside work with your boss, doing single-mom shit when you don't even got a kid?"*

That had been his response when I told him I couldn't accept his last-minute invite to an award show after-party because I already had plans to attend the City of Lights PTA fundraiser Suzie had spent months planning for her ten-year-old son.

I had told Dwayne about these plans. I even asked him to donate something to the raffle and come with me to the gala. He hadn't accepted my invite... or donated a single thing to the raffle... or taken it well when I'd chosen the event I'd already committed to over his thing. He'd just sent me another annoyed text:

> **"K. See ur choosing Suzie over me again."**

He also hadn't answered any of my texts after that until I told him I'd won the fundraiser's grand prize—an all-expenses-paid trip to Paris for two! He'd come around then and even hinted that he was working with the team's PR department to create a *super-special reel* for the L.A. Suns' social media account.

I'd been so excited, thinking about getting proposed to in Paris.

I'd never won anything in my life before that. And for a few months, while we waited for the end of the football season to take our possibly life-changing first trip abroad together, it felt like I was the luckiest woman in the world.

But look at me now.... Darkening the eggshell-colored armrest of my first-class seat with tears as we rose into the air at a 45-degree angle before settling into a straight line.

"Oh, for fuck's sake. I know sittin' next to me is overwhelmin', but this is too much."

What the...

My new seatmate's oddly cocky assumption stopped the tears I previously couldn't control like a faucet flipped down into the off position. In a flash, I went from crying inconsolably to glaring at—

The rolled white towel that he suddenly shoved into my eyeline before I could get a look at him. "Here, take this. It will help calm you down already."

My disgruntled frown lifted a little. Apparently, the flight attendant had handed warm towels out while I'd been crying, and he had gotten one for me.

Okay, thoughtful. But still, I had to ask, "What makes you think my crying has anything to do with you?"

He snorted. "You tryin' to tell me it's just a coincidence you started blubberin' on right when I had me a sit down next to you?"

"Not a coincidence exactly—" I started to say before stopping myself.

It wasn't like the real story was any less embarrassing than what the stranger was imagining.

Instead of explaining, I snatched the towel, pressed it into my face with both hands—and immediately forgave the cocky stranger for everything.

"Oh my God, you are you so right!" I admitted as the towel's heat seeped into my skin, loosening all the muscles I'd tightened during my crying fit. "This feels amazing!"

"Yeah, that heated towel's mint, that, ain't it?"

My new seatmate had an English accent, but not one of those nice, posh ones the British judges on American reality competition shows always seemed to have.

He'd dropped the "h" on "here" and "help," and just about all the "g"s on any word ending in -ing. His voice also had a gruff quality to it, one that didn't at all match the sophisticated dulcets I'd heard coming off the other English passengers in first class.

The cocky-but-thoughtful stranger's accent made me think of less of British judges who thought they knew everything and more of English crime shows featuring violent gangsters.

"So why all the tears, then, if it's not cos of me?" he asked. "You got a hate on that bad for planes."

I sacrificed the soothing towel for what was supposed to be a glance—just a quick peek to see who I was even talking to.

But then I couldn't tear my eyes away.

I thought the stranger in 1B only spoke like he could star in one of those violent British gangster shows. I didn't expect him to look like he could, too.

He wasn't bald, but his hair was shaved extremely close to his head. And even though he didn't appear to be that much older than me, his brutal face told a story of way more life experience. He had a crooked nose that had obviously been broken at least once, I could only assume in a fight. And his piercing black eyes locked onto mine with unnerving focus. I also noticed he wasn't dressed nicely, like the other mostly European men in first-class. He wore a simple gray tee and black jeans.

However, none of this made him unattractive. Other than the nose, his face was composed of sharp symmetrical lines. And I couldn't help but let my eyes roam over the biceps that hilled underneath the cuffs of his plain t-shirt before rolling into his forearms, both of which were heavily tattooed and roped with muscle.

No, he might not be dressed as nicely, but his strong, muscular build outdid every other man in first class.

Yeah, yeah, I saw it now.

Why the flight attendant had called me lucky when he showed up at the last minute to be seated next to me.

This guy oozed potent masculinity, and now I completely understood why he'd assumed I'd been so overwhelmed by the sight of him that I had burst into tears.

"Um, no, I actually like planes," I answered, awkwardly trying my best to recover—not just from the embarrassing crying jag but also from the sight of him.

He gritted his jaw and glared toward the window beside my seat. "Well, I don't like 'em. Don't like to be driven 'round by other people 'less I'm on the ground, and a lot of times not even then. And don't even get me started on takeoff and landin'."

He rolled his shoulders back. "Fuck, we both need a drink, don't we?"

It was technically a question, but his gruff voice made it seem more like a command.

I glanced nervously at the security notifications lit up above our seats. "Um, I don't think they can serve drinks before the fasten seatbelt lights go off."

"Naw, we're a'right." He waved down the flight attendant who'd called me lucky earlier and made a flipping motion with his hand, pantomiming throwing back a drink.

And I guess we were *alright*. What couldn't have been even two minutes later, the flight attendant came over to our seats with two glasses of champagne for us. And they were not only delivered with a smile, but also with a sexy wink for my seatmate, despite her wedding ring.

"You're happier now, right?" he asked after we'd both drained our flutes.

I thought about his question, blinked, and found myself realizing out loud, "Yeah.... Yeah, I actually feel a lot better."

"All fixed, then." He set the champagne glass aside like a judge pounding a gavel. "My job here is done."

I couldn't help but laugh. "So, you're one of those guys that's good at fixing things?"

He paused and squinted at me.

"I just... I just mean... I was such a mess a few minutes ago. And you seemed to know exactly what to do...."

I trailed off, heat crawling up my neck. Years of trying to wedge myself into the role of football player's girlfriend, and I still couldn't make small talk to save my life. Though, to be fair, neither Dwayne nor any of the other players on the L.A. Suns were as brutally hot as the guy currently squinting at me.

"I happen to come from a long line of electricians." He turned all the way sideways in his seat to face me with a grin that only lifted one side of his mouth. "Five generations for the power company, includin' me dad, me granddad, and all me uncles."

"Oh... wow. That's so cool." I let out the awkward breath I hadn't realized I was holding. "It's so nice that you've followed in their footsteps—and that I got to meet someone else in first-class who also isn't filthy rich."

A long pause. Then he turned his head and muttered something that sounded a lot like, "American. Should've guessed."

"Oh wow, I'm so sorry. Did I...?" The cheek-burning embarrassment came back for round two as I dipped my chin to ask, "Did I do or say something to offend you?"

Already? I silently added.

All the other folks in the Suns' payroll office who'd been to Europe had given me a long list of "Ugly American" things not to do. That was pretty much the only reason I'd opted to wear a skirt and a casual blazer instead of pair of leggings and my favorite yellow hoodie in first class.

I scoured my mind, trying to figure out what I'd said to make my British seatmate mutter under his breath. Maybe it was the comment about not being filthy rich? Yeah, that had to be it. I inwardly cringed, remembering how far Dwayne had gone to make it appear like he had way more money than he did. Ugh, I should have known better.

But then, instead of telling me off, he leaned in and rested his strong forearm on our shared armrest. "So, say you had something sparkin' off in your flat, somethin' that would be dangerous for you to manage by yourself. You could ring me, and I would come 'round, and yeah, love, I'd fix it. I'd fix whatever you wanted me to handle, whenever you needed it."

Wait, is he...

My thoughts faltered. Then canted to the side.

Was this brutally hot guy in first class *flirting*?

With me?

No, it couldn't be. Guys who looked like him didn't flirt with women who looked me. I mean, guys, in general, didn't come on to me. Ever.

I'd been the one to shyly offer to show Dwayne around L.A. four years ago because he said I reminded him of the girls back in his hometown of St. Louis after I helped him sort out a problem with his first paycheck.

That was what I was. All I was. A nice, helpful girl. Wholesome to my core.

So no, this obvious bad boy with a skin-fade haircut and what looked like a permanent five o'clock shadow couldn't possibly be flirting with me.

Could he?

As if to answer my question, 1B leaned even farther forward. So close his masculine scent filled my nose. Aggressively just soap and nothing else.

"Why were you askin' after my background, then, love? You got somethin' that needs fixin'?"

CHAPTER 2

Kayla

OKAY, EVEN I COULDN'T DENY THAT SEXUAL INNUENDO.

"No, I don't have anything that needs..." Forget my cheeks. My entire face was burning now. "I wasn't trying to... I was honestly just asking because, quite frankly, I don't belong here. I won this trip, you see. And since you appear... appear to not belong here, either, I was just wondering about your background. That's all."

He dragged his eyes up and down my face, obviously not convinced.

Then he just stared at me in a way that felt like getting completely dissected. But for the life of me, I couldn't bring myself to look away from his black gaze.

Luckily, the flight attendant chose that moment to reappear with more champagne. This time on a tray filled with flutes for everyone.

The stranger in 1B shifted his intense gaze away from me to accept another glass of bubbly from the flight attendant, and I could finally breathe again. Honestly, it felt like getting released from some kind of hypnotic trance.

"Yay, more champagne!" Trying to shake off the feeling that 1B had just straight-up stared into my soul, I all but snatched the flute of liquid courage from the attendant.

However, this time, instead of knocking back the alcohol, I leveled my voice and my rampaging thoughts enough to say, "Cheers. I'm Kayla, by the way."

Another long pause. Then: "You can call me Mick." He clinked his plastic flute against mine. "And yeah, cheers. Here's to movin' on."

I took a sip, but then had to ask, "Moving on?"

"That's what you're doin', right?" He leveled that direct gaze of his on me again. "Movin' on from the last guy? Why else would you be cryin' into your window if you don't bloody hate planes like meself."

I hesitated. The smart, practical payroll administrator inside of me was sending up all sorts of warning flares about getting too personal with some guy I'd just met on a plane.

But why not? I thought. The champagne felt nice and warm in my stomach, and I'd probably never see Mick again after the plane landed.

"Something like that," I admitted. "I was stupid enough to date a football player."

He regarded me with a confused squint. "You say you were datin' a football player, then?"

And I remembered, "Oh, you guys call soccer football. I forgot. I meant I was stupid enough to date an *American* football player. Do you know anything about American football?"

"Only that I'm bollocks at it," he answered.

"Well, I work as a payroll administrator for this American football team called the Los Angeles Suns."

Again with that up-and-down look. "You don't look like any money person I ever met. Guy who does up the money where I work has a pocket protector and a terrible hairpiece. Looks like a raccoon decided to make his final home up there. Know what I mean?"

I laughed. "We have a guy that looks exactly like that in our payroll office, too! It's actually a pretty unglamorous job. The only difference between our office and yours is that fifty-three of the employees we cut checks for happen to be football players. That's how I met my ex."

"The wanker who made you cry." His expression tightened in a way that reminded me of the old Clint Eastwood Westerns my dad loved to watch.

"Yeah, the wanker who made me cry." I couldn't help but laugh again.

"You said you won this trip to Paris." His expression softened. "Let me guess, it was a trip for two, and I took his seat. That was why you were cryin', right? Not because you were given the grand prize of gettin' to sit next to me for an hour plus."

I didn't know whether to laugh or ask him if he was being serious about assuming a grown woman would burst into overwhelmed tears just because he'd sat down next to her. Like, had that actually happened to him?

Though, if we're keeping it real, I wouldn't have been surprised if the answer to that question was yes. He'd only flirted with me a little, and I could barely keep it together. Imagine how someone—anyone from a less glamorous city than L.A.—

would have felt.

In the end, I decided to just answer Mick's question honestly. "No, it wasn't because of you. I don't even know you. But I was with my ex for four years. I thought we'd take this trip, and he'd finally propose...."

The memory of Suzie calling me into her office during her lunch hour three days ago rose up like a shadow in the back of my mind at the same time I decided to tell the stranger in 1B the entire bitter story.

"WHEN'S THE LAST TIME YOU TALKED TO DWAYNE?" Suzie asked as soon as I dropped down into one of her guest chairs after closing the office door behind me.

I blinked. Suzie always watched the latest episode of *Scuzz on TV* from 1:00 to 1:30 pm every weekday. She even had it blocked out on her calendar, just in case one of her staff got it in their head to schedule a meeting she'd have to attend at that time. I'd assumed she'd called me in to give me some breathless piece of gossip. But no...

"Not for a couple of weeks," I answered. "He's been super busy trying to secure investors for this nightclub idea of his during the off-season...."

I trailed off when the implications of Suzie's question—and the unusually grave look on her face—caught up with me. "Wait, why are you asking? Did something happen to Dwayne? Is he in trouble?"

"Look at you, worried about Dwayne first things first." Suzie shook her head. "You are too damn nice. I mean, just the best.

And, girl, I do not want to be the one to show you this. But you're my best friend, so..."

She turned around her computer monitor to display the video of the Scuzz.com newsroom, where their television show took place. Then she pushed play on the keyboard.

"So, Suns kicker Dwayne Thornhill narrowly avoided getting traded this season, but it looks like he decided to make a trade of his own...." One of the young reporters on screen was gossiping with Scuzz.com's much older editor in chief. "According to my sources, he'd been dating the same girl for, like, four years. Her name's like Katie or Kim or something...?"

"She famous?" The older editor cut off the young reporter before he could look up my name.

"Nope."

"Then her name doesn't matter." The editor in chief made a dismissive hand motion over the bill of his trucker hat. "What's going on with Thornhill? Get to it."

"Well, here's Thornhill last night at the Celebrity Weekly after-party for the Stadium Awards.

The headline **HOT NEW COUPLE?** appeared over footage of Dwayne walking out of the party arm in arm with a heavily made-up woman. I immediately recognized her as one of the stars of *Sunset Sisters*—that reality show about four Hollywood socialite sibs who almost exclusively dated pro athletes.

"Hey, that's not Kim Nobody—that's Karly Kazian!" the editor in chief exclaimed over the footage.

My heart sank a little, but then I shook my head and reasoned, "This is probably just a publicity stunt."

"Oh, honey." Suzie's eyes filled with pity.

Still, I rushed to defend Dwayne. "No, no, seriously. He's looking for investors right now. He was probably pitching his club to her. I mean, they're just walking out of a party. It's not like they're actually—"

All of my justifications were interrupted by more footage—this time of Dwayne tonguing down Karly Kazian in the front seat of his sports car. The sports car I'd help him pay the bill on the previous month because he'd "miscalculated" some expenses.

And that's how I found out my trip to Paris would not include an engagement ring.

Or Dwayne.

"I was such an idiot," I told Mick as I remembered all the pitying glances I'd gotten from my fellow Suns coworkers during the days leading up to my now solo vacation. "And I feel like even more an idiot for crying—in first class, of all places!"

"Yeah, you should feel like a right idiot for cryin'." To my surprise, Mick regarded me with a serious, completely unsympathetic look. "That wanker's not worth any of your tears. You know that. Don't you?"

Yes, I did know that. I mean, I even told myself the same thing earlier, before my crying jag. But somehow, when Mick said it, I understood the truth of how stupid it was to cry over Dwayne, to my core.

"You're right. You're totally right." I swallowed down the last of my champagne. "And even more importantly, I've learned my lesson. No more liars—and no more football players!"

I looked to Mick for another rough affirmation of what I already knew. But instead of agreeing with me again, he shifted in his seat, and a long, uncomfortable silence followed my declaration.

Aw, geez. My cheeks heated with the uncomfortable realization that I'd been going on and on about my ex for way too long. Like, I'd told him the whole drawn-out story in excruciating detail. What was I thinking? This probably wasn't his idea of good—or even decent—conversation.

I reset, and this time, I was the one who turned to fully face him. "Enough about me, though. How did you come to be in first class, listening to me whine about my ex-boyfriend?"

He gave me a considering look before answering with a proud smirk. "Guess I won a trip, too. All expenses paid, including a room at the Tourmaline Paris. But I only got four days and three nights, so I won't be in Paris as long as you."

"Wow, the Tourmaline! That's one of the most expensive hotels in Paris, right? I had to use points to get my coach flight upgraded, and they're putting me up at a Benton Budget."

I let out a totally jealous sigh. "But you won, like, a truly luxurious trip. And you're choosing to take it alone? No girlfriend or bestie? I would have dragged my mom or my best friend, Suzie, along with me if I could have. But Mom couldn't get the time off, and my best friend has a ten-year-old son."

Mick shrugged. "Never been one for travel companions anyways. Learned to value alone time early in life, guess you could say. I'll probably spend most of the trip in front of me laptop, catching up on *Coronation Street* and whatnot."

I stared at him, at a total loss for what to say.

"That's an English drama," he explained, obviously mistaking the reason for my confused look. "I think you call 'em soap operas or something like that."

"But it's *Paris*. I can't believe you'd want to waste such a nice trip watching stuff on your computer. In fact, just the thought of you spending four days inside your hotel room makes me feel really sad for you. I mean, it's the City of Lights! There's so much to do. Think of all the sights you'll be missing."

He crooked his head to the side, and half his mouth lifted into something between a grin and a smirk. "Only sights I want to see in Paris are right in front of me and currently all covered up."

I stared at him for few seconds and then snorted. "Oh, I get it now. You're not serious, right? You're just playing with me."

I felt a little rude for laughing, but c'mon. Things like this just did not happen to me.

Yes, I was cute with some work. I knew that. Dwayne had been forever on me about how good I could look if I just tried harder.

But even at my most made-up, I didn't look like the kind of woman a guy like Mick would want to see naked.

He had to be joking. More giggles rose up like champagne bubbles in my chest. I mean, he had to be. Right?

"I'm not kiddin', Kayla." The grin disappeared from his face, and his voice suddenly turned serious. Very, very serious.

Oh.... wow....

My laughter died abruptly, replaced by shock and something else that had me raising my hand to my throat with a sudden wish for pearls to clutch.

"But we only just met," I whispered.

"Tell you what." That intense look reappeared in his black eyes. "You got four nights in Paris. Agree to spend the first one of 'em with me, and I'll make it memorable. I promise you that, Kayla. I'll rock your world. I'll rock your entire universe, if you let me."

My mouth parted on a silent gasp. *My entire universe? Is he serious?*

"I'm completely serious, love." He answered my question as if I'd spoken it out loud. He leaned in again, and those black eyes of his kept mine magnetized with frightening ease. "One night. That's all I'm askin'. All you have to do is say yes."

CHAPTER 3

Mick

"Thank you, but no. I don't think so." The pretty woman sitting beside me squirms under my gaze. "I'm kind of flattered. And a little intrigued, if I'm being honest. But I'm just not the kind of woman who does what you apparently want to do with someone I've just met. Sorry. And thank you again. But, um, no...."

Alright, the answer was no.

Reckon I should've seen that coming.

The memory of Eunice Baker giving me what for cos I dared to think I had a chance with her crept back like a rank stench in back of my mind.

"Bleeding hell, I'm not looking to snog you, Andy. I only took this gig tutoring you because my mum felt sorry for you with your home life and all that. But that doesn't mean I'm up for anything else with you. As if!"

That had been about a year or so before I signed my youth contract with FC Greenwich at the age of sixteen. Before I reached my full height of 6 foot 1. Before I'd even had a shag for the first time. Back in those days, I wasn't the Atomic Foot. I was just that daft lad, Andrew Michael Atwater. A proper ace on the pitch, but barely able to pass my maths at school.

I shouldn't have reckoned on Eunice giving us a nod when I went in for a kiss. And, I suppose, I shouldn't have expected Kayla to say yes to a one-nighter.

Could I even pull a nice bird without her clocking who I was? Turns out, the answer to that little thought experiment was no.

I tore my gaze away from Kayla and sunk back into my own seat, my chest caving in with disappointment. Should have thought that one through before "shooting my shot," as they say in the States.

Truth was, it had been donkey years—over a decade, actually— since I'd encountered someone who had no clue who I was.

Didn't travel that much outside of England unless it had something to do with footy matches. Every now and then, some brand would overlook my bad reputation and jet me off somewhere for an ad shoot as part of some endorsement deal. And here and there, I'd pop over to other countries to check in personally on some of my venture capital firm's earliest investments. You know, like the robotics start-up GoNoTo in the States and that Scottish fintech firm AlgoFortune.

A fair few Atwater Ventures investments had paid off handsomely during the fourteen years I'd been "betting on the future" of tech. But those two were the ones that made the letter "M" turn into a "B" behind the number of my self-worth in pounds.

"Welcome to the Ruthless Magnates Club!" Max Benton, my best —really my only—friend had welcomed me to the billionaire life after I landed the cover of *The New Entrepreneur*. Then he'd convinced me to meet him at his club in Mallorca to celebrate my success off the pitch.

Even in his posh nightclub packed with A-list celebs, not a single bird I spoke to needed an introduction. Hell, most of them made the move on me.

I'd figured Eunice Baker was a one-off of my younger days. Since becoming a proper adult, I hadn't been the kind of guy that had to hunt. Or even flirt.

Or so I thought.

This lass in 1A was proving me well wrong.

I might just be the only single straight bloke in history to wish I wasn't sitting next to a cute, interesting girl on a bloody plane.

Her gaze was gentle as heather. But it hit me like a lorry when she finally stopped sobbing and looked up from the hand towel I gave her. And I found myself more than liking the way she looked.

She had creamy brown skin, just a few shades lighter than her pretty dark-brown eyes, and a hairstyle I couldn't give a proper describe. Not braids, like the older woman at the FC Greenwich office's front desk. Not quite dreads, like some of my teammates. She wore her hair in soft, shoulder-length twists, instead of the long extensions I'd become used to from women of all colors in my circle.

My hands itched with the urge to reach up and touch them. Touch her...

Gazing down at her that first time, I wondered how she would react if I grabbed those soft twists and gave them a right hard tug. While whispering in her ear about all the dirty things I had in store for that sweet body of hers.

I couldn't help but wonder, couldn't stop meself from gawping at her like a proper nutter.

Truth is, I quite enjoyed staring at her.

I liked the way her own eyes widened when she got a proper look at me and how her chin dipped with concern when I mentioned I wasn't keen on planes. And don't even get me started on the shite my chest did when she shyly told me I was good at fixing things.

She struck me as even lovelier now that I'd gotten to know her a bit. She was easy to watch, like a telly. This lass wasn't like the hard silk birds who usually came my way, hoping for a shag as rough as I look. Every emotion she felt during our chat flashed across her face, bright as a neon sign.

So, when she shot me down, I could tell exactly what she was thinking about my proposal to continue our conversation horizontally in my hotel room.

Right, then. I took that as my cue to stop talking and go back to doing what I planned before her tears got to me. For a long, uncomfortable time, I sat there in silence, pretending like the woman in seat 1A didn't exist.

But, to my surprise, she picked back up the conversation thread like we hadn't both already said all there was to say.

"I mean, we only just met. Less than an hour ago, when I was crying like a fool."

In an instant, I was back to staring at her. Gotta admit, I also liked her voice. It was warm as honey, and it became hushed and uncertain whenever she got a bit nervous. When's the last time I got to talk with a quiet lass? Usually, they'd be as loud as possible, doing everything, including giving me a flash of their bits, just to grab my attention.

But Kayla wasn't like that. She didn't cover up her feelings. Didn't get all grabby grabby with my attention. Didn't try to make me believe she was someone other than exactly who she was. She was…

Honest.

The word rushed through my mind like a gust of spring wind.

Stop starin' at her, the voice of reason chided inside my head.

I averted my eyes, only to have them snap right back to her. Yeah, she was an open book—a book with a cute cover that I couldn't stop reading for some reason.

"You never done this, then? Never spent the night with someone you just met?"

I already knew the answer to that question. But I needed conversation cover to excuse how I was staring her down like a right creeper.

She fretted her bottom lip. "When I was in middle school, I had a spontaneous sleepover with a new girl who had just moved to our neighborhood. We watched *Mean Girls.* I really liked it, but I fell asleep halfway through."

Unlike Kayla, I had no problem keeping how I was really feeling behind a stone façade. But at that instant, I had to suck in my abs to hold back a laugh.

"Tell ya what." I schooled my face back to serious. "I can promise a night with me will be the opposite of that middle school sleepover."

She smiled at my new pull line. But then opened her mouth for what I could tell was about to be another polite no.

"Sorry, Mick-o," she might say. *"Good girls like me don't agree to hook up with bad boy strangers like you."*

I roamed my eyes over her features one last time, knowing this would probably be the last chance I got to do so before the incoming rejection.

"Thank you for inviting me to your hotel room, even after that embarrassing crying jag." Her polite letdown came down the tunnel just as expected as the first train of the morning from Manchester to London. "That was super sweet of y—"

"La machine hôte redescendre a débuté venir gagner...."

Kayla cut off to listen to the pilot's landing announcement, delivered in French first, then in English.

As soon as the pilot wrapped up the usual instructions about returning our seats to the upright position and buckling up for the descent, she swiveled back toward me, her eyes brimming with concern.

My stomach tightened for reasons that had nothing to do with our sudden descent into Paris. Did she really reckon my pride was so fragile that I couldn't handle her incoming rejection?

"Yeah, I knew this would be hard for you."

Forget concern. Now she was looking at me with straight-up pity.

Alright, maybe it was. I clenched the armrest, knuckles gone white. Couldn't say I was fond of this empty pit in my chest as the bloody plane started its descent.

But, determined not to let on how I was feeling, I kept my face stony.

But then, she somehow managed to slide her hand underneath mine on the armrest. "Here, just hold on to me. It will be over before you know it."

That was when it hit me that she hadn't been talking about turning down my offer again, but about my fear of planes.

All my annoyance faded away when I realized she was giving me something other than a cold hunk of metal to hold on to as I got through my least favorite part of flying.

She'd remembered. She remembered that little thing I mentioned about hating flying at the start of our chat.

I was a grown man. A pro-footballer known throughout the worlds as one the meanest and nastiest players on the pitch.

But she was right. I despised flying. Hated not being in control and the fear that came with letting someone else take the wheel—in the bloody sky, of all places.

With a thundering heart, I took her gift, gripping her hand tight as we descended, then finally bumped to the ground.

"Oh, yay, we made it safely." Her voice soothed my nerves better than the shots of whiskey I usually knocked back before the descent ever could.

And when she turned her head to smile at me, it felt like the first glimpse of spring sunshine after a too-long English winter. My heart slowed, filling with an emotion I couldn't quite pin a name to.

"Don't worry. It's all over."

It's all over. Those three words froze everything she had warmed up inside my chest.

I was a world-famous footballer, always in the top five on *The Sport Review*'s annual Hottest Footballer Bachelors list. Walk into any club in Paris tonight, I'd not only get the VIP treatment but my pick of any woman I wanted.

But I didn't want any of those women.

Kayla. The woman who'd interrupted her rejection to hold my hand on the way down, that was who I wanted. More than anyone or anything else right now.

"It doesn't have to be over." No more Mr. Smooth. My voice came out guttural, with a faint hint of desperation—something I hadn't felt since I was sad Andrew Michael Atwater, still living with the shitty set of parents I was determined to shed when I signed on with FC Greenwich.

I felt embarrassed for myself. But I couldn't bring myself to let go of her hand. Couldn't stop myself from staring her down as I all but pleaded, "Don't say no, Kayla. It doesn't have to be over. Meet me at my hotel after you're all sorted in yours. One night. One night is all I'm askin'."

She stared back at me, her expression filled with shock—probably because I was coming off like a right nutter.

And even though I already knew what her answer would be, my heart thundered in my chest, even louder and harder than it did on the descent.

So loud, I could barely hear her when said, "Okay, why not? I never do this. Never let myself just live. So yes. Yes, I'll meet you at your hotel tonight. Let's have ourselves a one-night stand."

CHAPTER 4

Mick

"This way, Monsieur Atwater, please."

A French butler, decked out in a smart navy suit, flung open the doors to the Tourmaline Paris Étoile's poshest penthouse suite with more flourish than I personally thought was needed for the occasion.

Especially since I had to hang back while the whole place got a once-over from the guard/driver the Paris Triomphe FC sent to pick me up at the airport.

Couldn't say I blamed him for the extra vigilance. The Tourmaline was a top choice for celebrities and bigwigs with high-level security needs. But ultras—as we called the footie fanatics—could be crafty. The lasses, especially.

Been surprised more than once by a stark-naked girl waiting for me on the bed, like I'd ordered her up from room service. So, I was chuffed when the guard came back out to the hallway empty-handed. No "presents" from the fans—or, even worse, a "Gree-nie," those special brand of ultras that worshiped at the altar of FC Greenwich.

That shite was the last thing I needed with Kayla due to rock up any minute.

Speaking of which...

"Oi, we all sorted for my special guest?" I asked the butler, whose name I'd already binned from my head.

"Oui, monsieur. I shall personally escort Madame Edwards here upon her arrival and refer to you solely as Monsieur Atwater, omitting any personal details, as per your request. Additionally, be assured that everything else you asked for will be ready to go as soon as you give the signal."

If he was weirded out by my instructions, it didn't show. His wrinkled face didn't let on nothing as he confirmed everything I'd told him to do.

I gave him a nod, feeling chuffed. Maybe more than I ought of considering the last-minute arsehole tactic I'd pulled to make sure Kayla didn't flake on our one-nighter.

But it wasn't like she'd left me with a load of options, was it?

KAYLA HAD SAID YES TO MY INDECENT PROPOSAL WHEN we touched down, but once the seatbelt light went off, she went fidgety and started up with all the "um... um... um..." business again.

That American neon-sign face of hers clued me in that something negative was going on inside her head. I could tell she was already talking herself out of the "okay, yes" she'd given me earlier.

Did I let on that I knew she was having second thoughts, though? Nah, not a chance.

I reached up to fetch her hand luggage down from the overhead for her, all considerate-like, acting like our plan was still a done thing in both her head and mine.

"I'll be waitin' here 'til everybody's off the plane to disembark meself," I told her, smooth as you like, handing over her bag. "But no worries, we'll be seeing each other again later on at my hotel."

She made a non-committal noise and gripped the handle of her luggage like it was some sort of lifeline. "Thanks for talking me down on the flight. I'm really glad I met you."

Kayla put a note of finality in her voice, like she was saying her goodbyes.

She didn't suss out who I truly was, did she?

Didn't understand I wasn't the sort of lad to let a lass like her slip away. Even when she got nervous.

But she'd find out soon enough.

"Remember, I'm over at the Tourmaline," I carried on, grinning down at her like we were in full agreement. "Top floor. Penthouse suite. Only one of 'em at the Tourmaline, far as I know."

"Okay, the Tourmaline..." She was practically retreating down the aisle toward the airplane's entrance now.

"Name's Mick—Mick Atwater," I called after her. "Don't forget."

"Yes, I'll remember," she answered, still shuffling down the aisle.

"And what's your full name?" Something devilish in me wanted to keep on toying with this little mouse who had no clue she was being chatted up by a lion. A lion who would stop at nothing to get what he wanted. *Who* he wanted. "Gotta drop it at the front desk."

She paused, her shoulders tightening underneath the knee-length winter coat she'd slipped on while I fetched her suitcase. Then she turned back around to answer, "Kayla. My full name is Kayla Edwards, and no matter what happens, Mick..."

Her pretty brown eyes filled with unspoken apology as she regarded me over the handle of her roller board. "It was... um... so nice meeting you. Please believe that. Goodbye, Mick."

This time she said her goodbye out loud.

But I didn't say it back.

Just watched her turn the corner and vanish from sight.

Knowing full well that I would not be letting her go.

Not that easy.

And, not just yet

I DIDN'T WASTE ANY TIME GAWPING AT THE PENTHOUSE after I was given the all-clear to step inside the rooms that would be my digs for the next four days.

When your best mate's a scion of a multi-billion-dollar hotel family, you end up in your fair share of penthouse suites. And once you've seen one of those over-the-top dealios, you've pretty much seen them all.

So, I strolled into yet another massive hotel suite, and it was the same old song and dance. Wall of glass stretching from one end of the room to the other. Only difference was, outside the windows, the sun was setting over a city view that included the Seine and the Eiffel Tower.

The rest of the room was cut from the same cloth as pretty much every penthouse hotel suite in Europe.

Fancy gold-etched plasterwork everywhere, plush furnishings covered in rich fabrics, separate sleeping quarters with a colossal bed, and art on the wall worth more than the standard starting salary of most footy players.

A crystal chandelier hung from an ornate white ceiling over a large, round dining table, and on top of it sat a massive vase of flowers with a note card attached.

I had no doubt who they were from, but I moseyed over to the table to read the card anyhow.

"Shall I be of assistance with the unpacking of your suitcase, monsieur?" the French butler asked behind me.

"Nah, you can bugger off, mate. Just sort out the rest, like I told you," I answered as I eyeballed the card.

Yeah, the flowers were from Coach Ollie, just as I guessed.

Welcome to Paris, Atwater. Hope to send over a Paris Triomphe jersey with your name on the back soon.

Well, isn't that a sweet gesture? I thought—before balling up the note and chucking it into the nearest bin. Then I glanced around the room, making sure there weren't any more clues about my real identity lying about for Kayla to stumble upon.

There weren't. It was just me, all alone in a hotel room big enough to fit an entire family.

"But it's Paris!"

Kayla's words echoed through my mind as I ambled over to the window to take in the view that would be backdropping my stay.

"... Just the thought of you spending four days inside your hotel room makes me feel really sad for you. I mean, it's the City of Lights! There's so much to do. Think of all the sights you'll be missing."

My one-nighter with Kayla was only a game, I told meself. A bit of lion and mouse play that I knew I'd win.

But, for some reason, the hollow ache inside my chest just wouldn't bugger off already.

All this luxury. And no one to share it with. The gloomy thought popped into my head out of nowhere.

Only to be interrupted by my private phone vibrating in the pocket of my leather bomber jacket.

It was Max. I answered the call with a deep frown.

"Oi, mate. Why're you ringin' me instead of textin'?"

"I figured you wouldn't want to text about the American girl you were flirting with on the plane," Max answered on the other side of the line.

"How the bloody hell—" I started to ask.

But Max interrupted before I could finish. "C'mon, you know first class gets all the attention on the socials. Check out what No1GreenieFlame132 posted."

Max read aloud, "Heartbreak emoji. 'Spotted @AtomicAtwater with some American girl in first class on the way to Paris. Does this mean I'll never get my chance?' More heartbreak emojis. Like, a whole row of them."

Max let out a dry chuckle. "From the look of this blurry back-of-the-heads pic Number1GreenieFlame236 snuck, you and this American chick were getting real cozy in the front seats."

"Did they figure out who she is?" I asked with a guilty heart, thinking of what Kayla had just gone through with her wanker ex.

"Not yet. That's why I'm calling you."

I breathed a sigh of relief. Luckily, she was American. She probably wouldn't even clock it if her image ended up on some European footie gossip site. Still, I didn't want anyone harassing her because of me.

"So, who is she?" Max asked again. "It's not like you to go on vacation with some anonymous woman—or go on vacation, period, unless I harass you into it. Is this American the reason you decided to finish up your holiday break in Paris instead of coming to Mykonos to party with me?"

My dark mood lightened a bit. "Nah, not really. But now that you guessed it, I'm glad for the cover story."

Since it was Max, I let him in on the real deal. "Got some contract negotiations comin' up with the Old Green, and you know Cedric Oliver—he was one of the assistant coaches for FC Greenwich before he got the head coachin' gig for this French team. Anyway, Coach Ollie's been sniffin' around with a Paris Triomphe contract. Said the salary raise would be '*more* than competitive.' His words, not mine."

"I bet. Triomphe's the club owned by the Middle Eastern family behind the Tourmaline Group, right?" Max lets out an impressed whistle. "Hotels, planes, soccer teams. Their big-oil money makes the Benton Brand look like a mom-and-pop motel."

"Yeah, that's right. Figured I'd use their hefty offer in euros to squeeze more quid out of Greenwich."

"If it's all about leverage, why use this American as cover, then?" Max's tone shifted from curious to puzzled. "Don't you *want* FC Greenwich to know Paris is interested?"

"I want 'em to know *durin'* the salary negotiations. Not a month beforehand, when they've got time to replace me with two up-and-comers whose combined salaries won't be nearly as much as what my agent's plannin' to ask 'em for to keep me around. If I want Old Green to pay what I'm worth, I'll be needin' an offer from France for 'em to outbid, won't I?"

"Okay, I get it now. Should have known you wouldn't change up overnight for some American chick." Max's voice turned relieved and filled with admiration. "You're playing all the angles. Getting laid and setting yourself up to get paid at the same time. Nice."

Not nice, actually.

A slimy feeling crawled over me when he put it like that.

Max didn't know about the instant connection I'd felt with that "American chick."

Or about the hollow ache in my chest.

"Hey, I'm still partying in Greece. I'm practically next door." Max's voice brought me back to the current convo. "But I opened a new club in Paris a few months ago. Maybe I'll hop on the jet and join you. Fuck that World's Worst CO_2 Emissions List I made last year. Again."

The doorbell rang before I could answer.

"Mick? Mick? You still there?" Max said into my ear, calling me by the name reserved for my inner circle of friends and business mates.

"Talk later," I told Max. Then I hung up before he could respond

Kayla was here.

Somehow, I knew it even before I opened one of the suite's doors and found her on the other side, standing beside the French butler.

He wore an eager expression, at the ready to serve. Like every butler in every fancy hotel on the planet Earth.

But Kayla's adorable face was full-on furious.

Before I could even say hi there, how's it goin', she demanded, "Tell me you didn't steal my luggage and have it delivered here!"

CHAPTER 5

Kayla

"Hey there, love. Dead chuffed you could make it."

Instead of assuring me he didn't steal my luggage, Mick gave François, the butler who escorted me up to his room, a hand signal that made the older man back away with a discreet nod and disappear down the hallway.

"How's it goin', then?" Mick leaned against the doorjamb and folded his arms over his zipped-up leather bomber jacket once François was gone.

Then he gave me a slow up-and-down look. His seductive gaze raised goose bumps on my skin, despite it being warm and toasty in the hallway outside his suite.

Good God, why did he have to be so stupidly hot? It really was just incredibly unfair. Especially under these circumstances.

"How's it goin', then?" I repeated, more than a little flustered. "Not great, actually! I waited for eons for my suitcase, only to find out it had already been claimed and brought to the Tourmaline! What the heck, Mick? Do you have it or not?"

"Yeah. Thought, since you said yes to meetin' up with me, I'd have the airport guy grab your bag, too."

Any expectation of an apology that I'd carried up in the private elevator with me died on his careless shrug. There wasn't a hint of contrition on Mick's face or a note of remorse in his voice.

"You wanna come in?" He hitched a thumb over his shoulder. "It's 'round here... somewhere."

"Oh, wow, I can't believe you!" To say I was furious would've been an understatement. I pushed past him into his hotel room. "You just took my luggage, and you didn't even bother to tell—oh, whoa, what is this?"

I broke off ranting, and my mouth fell open when I got ahold of Mick's penthouse suite. "Seriously?! This is the suite you won? It looks like something out of a magazine spread. Not real place where human beings are actually allowed to live!"

I rushed to the floor-to-ceiling windows, where the sun was setting over the Seine and the Eiffel Tower, like it was posing for a post-card. "I can barely believe it is real. I mean, look at this view!"

"Yeah, look at the view. It's beautiful...."

I didn't realize Mick had followed me over to stand in front of the landscape windows until I turned to find him...

Staring at me, as opposed to the sparkling view.

My heart stuttered. But then I remembered the reason I was standing in front of this picture-perfect view instead of settling into my own hotel room.

"Why did you do that?" I turned to face him with a shake of my head. "Why did you steal my luggage without telling me?"

"Didn't have your number," he answered. "Or I certainly would have dropped you an SMS. Hindsight being 20-20, reckon we should've thought of exchangin' digits before we got off the plane."

He shook his head woefully, as if all of this could have been avoided if either of us had thought to offer up our phone numbers.

I glared at him. "You expect me to believe this was just a simple miscommunication and not some evil plan to make sure I didn't back out of our one-night stand?"

He raised both eyebrows in a way that would have made me look cartoonish. But, of course, the look came off as even more sinfully handsome on him. "Were you planning to back out of our one-nighter without telling me, then?"

"I... um... well... I..." His direct question put me on the unexpected defense. But in the end, I confessed, "Okay, not going to lie, I was having second thoughts."

I winced. "The thing is, I'm a very practical person. I've had a regular eight-to-five job since graduating from community college. I live below my means and with my parents because it's cheaper. I drive an economy sedan, and I always pay my bills on time. Seriously, I've only done three impractical things in my entire life."

I ticked the items off on my fingers. "Number one was asking out a professional football player because I was tired of swiping left and I thought he truly was a nice Midwestern boy at heart. Two was taking this trip, and that was only because I won it in a raffle."

I got that this explanation did not make me come off as sexy in any way, shape, or form. But that was kind of the point.

Once I was on a roll with my explanation about why I'd been rethinking our one-night stand, the rest spilled out like word vomit. "Plus, I had two glasses of champagne on the plane. And you know, in America, they suggest giving it an hour per unit of alcohol before getting behind the wheel. No offense but…"

I shook my head at him and gave it to him straight. "You are a huge wheel. Like the kind you find behind those extremely dangerous monster trucks my little brother loves. So, I was like, *Here's the plan, Kayla. Go back to your hotel room and take at least a couple of hours to make your final decision. That way, you'll know for sure that you're in your right mind*. Because this is kind of crazy, right?"

I waggle my hands between us. "You and me are not your usual swipe right kind of situation. In fact, I'd bet my entire 401k that I'm nothing like the women you're used to one-night-standing."

I trailed off into nervous silence, hoping he'd put me out of my misery, give me my suitcase back already, and send me on my way to continue living my boring, practical life.

But instead of letting of me off the hook, he asked, "What's the third thing, then?"

"Excuse me?"

He regarded me with a lazy gaze. Like a cat toying with a mouse. But not a regular house cat.

More like a lion. In a dangerously hot British man's clothing.

He clarified his question. "What's the third nutty thing you've done in your otherwise dead, practical life?"

My heart beat in my throat, and I had to swallow it down to admit, "Saying yes to you on the plane."

A weird, pained look came over his face. As if I'd kicked him.

"I'm sorry," I rushed to say. "I didn't mean to insult you. I'm just trying to be honest."

He shook his head. "That's the thing, love. I'm not used to that from women."

"Being insulted?"

"Honesty." His eyes roamed over my face, like I was some math problem he couldn't quite figure out. "I'm not used to women— anyone, really—just being completely honest with me. It's a little overwhelmin', if we're exchangin' truths right now."

"Overwhelming." A snort of laughter escaped before I could stop it. "That's a great word for it. Now you know how I feel every time I interact with you."

"Now I know." He laughed, too, but it was a quiet sound. And his eyes remained serious as he continued to stare down at me.

"You... um..." I swallowed again as the rays of the setting sun bathed the gorgeous hotel room in warm golden light. "You said something about getting my suitcase?"

"Yeah, I did. Earlier." He stepped forward, closing the space between us.

Making it so I had to crank my head back to keep from speaking into his chest when I said, "Well, I should probably grab it. All my stuff is in there. Including my e-reader with the latest Clara Quinn book. And I don't love reading on my phone, so..."

I waited for him to move away or at least point me toward my missing bag.

But he just stood there, unmoving, his leather and soap scent filling up my nose. Like a vintage song about the kind of guy you can want but never keep. "So, you're a massive Clara Quinn fan, eh?"

"Oh, yes. The hugest!" My excitement for The Fae Realm saga temporarily eclipsed my intent to get my luggage back. "She's my favorite author of all time, and it's been years since her last book. Do you know her?"

"Never heard of her, actually." He rubbed the back of his neck with an apologetic wince. "Don't read much meself. I'm more of an action movie guy."

"And that *Coronation Street* show you mentioned," I reminded him with a teasing smile.

He grinned. "Yeah, that series's mint, innit? Been watching since I was a kid. Reckon it will still be runnin' when I'm dead in the ground."

I tried to laugh, but found I couldn't.

It was such a silly conversation. Yet, tension crackled between us, like an electrified energy field that would shock me. If I dared to touch it.

I cleared my throat. "So, about my bag..."

"That's your plan, then?" His black eyes locked mine into his assessing gaze. "You're just gonna tail it back to your hotel room at the Benton Budget and wait for the booze to wear off until you're in your right head?"

"Yes." I gave him a nod that was way more determined than I actually felt. "Yes, that's my plan."

He stared at me for several long, intense moments. Then his face suddenly broke into a wide grin. "Right-o, then. You can stay here with me and have some scran while we wait out the champer's buzz."

Wait. What? "Oh, that's not what I meant—"

41

The suite's doorbell sounded before I could finish protesting.

"Yeah, come through, mate!" Mick called out, finally stepping back from me. "We're all ready for ya!"

I discovered then that "scran" apparently meant "dinner" when François entered with a man in a hotel worker uniform pushing a rolling cart, on top of which sat several trays covered in golden lids.

"Oh, my gosh, you ordered dinner?" Forget the sunset. I gaped at Mick now. "How much did that cost? You shouldn't have—"

Mick just shook his head. "Don't worry 'bout the cost, love. It's just dinner. One dinner. That's all you have to give me. Then you can knock off back to your Benton Budget setup if you want. Just don't make me eat alone in this posh hotel room."

He held out his hand with an almost comical pleading look. "C'mon, Kayla. One dinner. That's all I'm asking of you right now. Please, don't say no."

I glanced down at his extended palm, rough and covered in calluses.

Please, don't say no.

His words echoed in my head. Short-circuiting my good sense.

Maybe that's why, instead of taking his hand, I rose onto my tiptoes, braced my hands against his chest...

And tentatively kissed him instead.

CHAPTER 6

Kayla

IT WAS AN IMPULSE, REALLY.

A small test to assess whether I could actually handle intimacy with a complete stranger.

Handle *him*.

Nothing more than an innocent peck

But by the time I lowered back down to my heels, his entire face had changed. Those black eyes of his were no longer just studying me, asking me to please stay for dinner.

They *burned*. And I felt anything but innocent under his gaze.

Some life-preserving instinct made me step back. At least, I tried to step back.

His arm shot out before I could, wrapping around my waist and banding me to him.

A primal beat. Then: "Get out. Get out now."

He looked straight at me as he said this, making my heart jump. But I realized he wasn't talking to me when François responded, "Right away, Monsieur. Let us know if anything else is needed."

Mick didn't answer the butler. Just pulled me in even closer as he and the uniformed hotel worker hastily departed the room.

Mick's rigid length pressed into my stomach. Scaring me but somehow thrilling me at the same time.

Suddenly, my heart was beating so fast I felt a little breathless. As if I'd done an hour of cardio—not just briefly touched my lips to his.

"A'right, then," he said when the door closed behind François. "I'm assumin' the champagne's worn off?"

Maybe I should have lied. It felt like my heart was about to give out.

But, as we'd already more than established, I had a problem with being honest to a fault.

"It would seem so, yes," I confirmed on a choked whisper.

Another intense beat. We hadn't touched the food, but it felt like his gaze was eating me up for dinner.

"I want to kiss you." He brought a callused thumb up to my chin and stroked it under my bottom lip. "Can I kiss you?"

I hesitated. The timid payroll administrator inside of me warning of checks I might not be able to cash.

"Don't say no, Kayla." His hungry gaze dropped to my lips. "I'm fuckin' desperate for your mouth."

Don't say no, Kayla. There were those magic words again. Destroying my reason. Making me nod when I probably should have been running.

One nod was all he needed.

Mick's mouth crashed down onto mine, devouring me underneath his kiss.

A new fire licked through me, heating up everything below my waist. His lips were soft, but his kiss was rough. It knocked my head back, consuming me with desire.

That kiss was everything I never knew I wanted.

But eventually, it was no longer enough.

More. My fingers scrabbled at his leather bomber jacket. "*I want more.*"

I didn't realize I'd said that out loud until he roughly groaned my name and started removing clothes from my body.

His lips barely left mine, but before I knew it, both our jackets were gone. My top was pulled off over my head, and my broom skirt somehow ended up in a puddle on the floor.

This was moving so fast. *Too fast.*

But I could barely bring myself to care. The kiss had gone straight to my head. Even faster than the champagne.

But then, he abruptly ended it. Pulling back from me.

"Fuckin' hell. Look at you...."

He let out a harsh breath as his eyes roamed over my cotton kelly-green boy shorts and matching bra like they were the finest lingerie.

A wave of self-consciousness began to cool off the heat from our kiss. Yes, I'd wanted to feel him on my skin. But it was excruciating to watch him watch me like that.

I nervously raised my arms to cover my chest.

"No, Kayla, let me have my look." He gently knocked my arms back to my sides. And when I tried to raise them again, he wrapped his large, callused hands around my much smaller wrists. Pinning them there with what didn't appear to be much effort at all. As he continued to stare his fill.

For several moments on end, we just stood there—a still-life character study, like one of the paintings on the wall behind us. His large hands on my wrists. His dark eyes on my body.

"Window or floor?" he eventually asked.

My brow furrowed in confusion. "Um... Excuse me?"

A knowing and completely wicked grin spread across his face as he informed me, "We're not going to make it to the bedroom."

Then he asked again, his voice coarse with heat. "Window or floor?"

I swallowed nervously. This was not the kind of question I was used to getting asked—much less answering.

"How about the couch?" I countered, glancing at the sleek piece of gray furniture sitting just a few feet away.

"So, you want me to make the decision for you, that it?"

His tone was pleasant. But his smile turned feral.

"Seriously, the couch is right there. Why don't we just—oh!"

My back hit the window before I could finish making my argument, and his lips once again crashed into mine.

What am I protesting again? All practical thoughts flew out of my head. And I melted back into his kiss, my body becoming pliant against the cool glass as he unzipped his jeans and pulled something out of his back pocket.

A condom, I vaguely realized when I felt his rigid length press into my stomach again. This time sheathed in a thin layer of latex.

That was the last reasonable thought I got to have.

Mick cupped a hand around the back of my nape, pushing his tongue even deeper into my mouth as his fingers slipped below the waistband of my plain cotton panties to find my core.

Two digits pushed inside of me, working my below the same way his tongue was working my mouth.

The sensations were unbelievable.

I moaned into his kiss, and my folds clenched hard around his fingers as he moved them inside of me with masterful strokes. It felt so good to be touched like that while his mouth claimed mine.

There was no room to think. No space to feel any sort of way about the bullet train I suddenly found myself riding.

Toward sex.

Him. All I felt was him. All I wanted was this.

But then he broke off the kiss again. This time with a curse.

"You're already wet."

I blinked in confusion. *Is that a bad thing?*

"I promised you a good time, but I'm not going to be able to..."

He pulled his fingers out of me, and suddenly his hands were on the back of my thighs, lifting.

Never in my life had someone picked me up during a kiss.

But somehow, I instinctively knew what to do.

I wrapped my legs around his waist and my arms around his neck, holding on for dear life as he tugged aside the crotch of my boy shorts.

"Kayla!" He groaned into my mouth before taking me completely. With one forceful stroke that moved my entire body upward on the glass.

He was large! Not just long but also so thick my folds stretched and strained to accommodate him. It should have hurt. There'd been barely any foreplay beyond kisses.

But he'd been correct about how wet I was. It felt nothing but good to have him inside of me. Right. My core pulsed all around him, welcoming the pleasure of his invasion. Like he belonged there.

"You feel amazing," I told him on a happy sigh. "Thank you. Thank you for convincing me to do this."

I softly kissed his shoulder, excited for what was about to come next.

However, Mick just remained rigid inside of me. Holding me, but not moving. His breathing was harsh, and the corded back muscles underneath his t-shirt flexed and pulsed.

Like a bull trying to hold himself back.

"Mick?"

I'd meant for his name to come out like a concerned question, the equivalent of an "Are you all right?"

But my womanhood clenched around him as I said his name, turning it into a moan.

And that was it.

One moment, Mick was a statue, and the next, his hips had me pinned to the glass as he took me with powerful strokes. Ragged and brutal. But oh-so-good.

A knot of pleasure tightened inside of me, rolling my eyes. It felt like I was precariously balanced on a knife's edge of sensation. I clung to him, afraid to fall.

But then Mick dug in deeper, pressing the rough sandpaper of his five o'clock shadow into the space between my neck and shoulder. He drove into me, again and again, relentless in his attack.

No more balancing. I fell. Fell and fell until I exploded.

The land mines inside of us seemed to be connected. Mick came just seconds after my climax hit.

"Kayla!"

He let out a guttural yell as his body seized into mine, and he released into the condom.

A thick silence filled the air between us as our chests heaved in the aftermath of that sudden sex explosion.

Then we just stared at each other, his eyes as wide and shocked as I felt.

I got the feeling we were both wondering the same thing.

What was that?

CHAPTER 7

Mick

WHAT WAS THAT?

I still don't have a good answer for that question when Kayla emerges from the WC, freshly showered and dressed in a new outfit. She must've packed the fresh togs in her hand luggage.

I knew for a rather morally grey fact that her big bag was still in the downstairs lobby baggage claim with strict instructions to only be released to me.

"Wow, that bathroom is nicer than anything I've ever seen in a hotel before!" Kayla sat down at the dining table, where I'd set up the room service dinner while she rinsed off. "It had a separate claw-foot tub, too! Maybe you can have a nice soak while watching *Coronation Street*."

I just grunted and lifted the golden bell lids off the two plates of fancy French grub.

"Yer choice. You can have the chicken slathered in sauce or the veal slathered in sauce."

Kayla's eyes lit up at the sight of the gourmet dishes. "Ooh, they both look so delicious. But I'll take the chicken, if that's okay with you."

Nothing about this situation was okay with me. But I gritted my jaw and passed her the plate of chicken.

"I can't get over how much way nicer your prize package is than mine." Kayla gave the suite another admiring look as she unrolled her silverware from the cloth napkin. "I'm assuming you won that big Tourmaline Sweepstakes promotional event they were running over the holidays, right?"

"Yeah. Right." I unrolled my own set of cutlery out of its cloth napkin, deciding to keep my answers—and lies—short.

"Well, that's amazing. Congratulations." Kayla's voice sounded a little hesitant and a lot less enthusiastic now. "I mean, what are the odds of winning a huge prize package like that?"

"Not a clue."

"Okay, well..."

A silence, loud as stadium boos, fell over the meal as Kayla gave up trying to talk to me and awkwardly picked up her knife and fork.

I knew I was being a right twat.

If I'd been even half a gentleman, I'd have tried some small talk. But I couldn't bring meself to open my mouth and at least pretend I was a decent human being who could share a meal with a lovely woman without getting all up in his head about it.

The truth was, all my energy was going toward not looking how I felt.

Which was truly fucking rattled.

Prior to what happened earlier at the window, I'd thought I was the lion, luring the skittish American mouse into my den.

Yet there I sat, as unnerved as a rookie after losing a big game, just completely unable to wrap my head round how poorly I'd performed.

I'd intended to give Kayla a great time. Take her nice and slow after convincing her to commit to our one-nighter over a proper dinner.

Instead, she'd kissed me once, and I'd...

My stomach knotted at the memory of me rutting her against the window, unable to control meself. Like some sort of beast.

Where had the smooth international football star who'd slept with more than his fair share of women been then? Gone. That was where. Disappeared like that Frenchie butler as soon as I got a single taste of Kayla "I know I'm not your type" Edwards.

I angrily sawed off a piece of the veal scallopini and shoved it in my mouth.

Jesus Christ, it was still warm! I inwardly cursed meself for rushing through our first round with enough time left over for Kayla to take a shower without fear of having to eat a cold meal.

What must she think of me now? Mr. Big Talk about how I would rock her universe turning out to be little more than an animal who could barely control himself once he got inside her.

It was her body that did me in, if I'm being truthful. I'd not known what to expect, given the bulky nature of her T-shirt and skirt ensemble.

But underneath all that fabric, I'd found large and lovely breasts, Greek goddess hips, and a derriere so expansive it could barely be contained by the boy shorts she was wearing.

Kayla turned out to be the perfect package, wrapped up in a bright green underwear set. Like a gift of chocolate left over from the holidays. One I'd been excited to consume even after Christmas had long passed. *Too* excited.

I glowered sullenly across the table at her new outfit. It was even worse than the t-shirt and skirt ensemb.

A bulky L.A. Suns hoodie and a baggy pair of zebra-print sweats that hid even more of her delectable body.

Fuck me. Why, oh, why hadn't I taken the time to fully unwrap before pushing her into that window like some kind of depraved nutter? I hadn't even given meself the chance to see what her lush breasts looked like underneath that bra.

"Okay, well, thank you for dinner!" Kayla abruptly stood up and threw down her napkin. "It's time for me to go."

"Wait, we're not even done eatin'." I stood up, too, proper alarmed and dead confused.

"Yeah, I think we're all done here." She threw me a right-irritated look over our half-eaten food. "When you ordered dinner, I thought, I don't know, that you actually wanted to share a meal with me. But you're barely talking, and I can see now you were just being nice and that I should have left after we..."

She rubbed her hand over her forehead, her irritated look turning into one of pained embarrassment. "Listen, I haven't dated in a really long time—not that we're dating. Oh God, I'm so not good at this. I'm sorry. I'm just going to go, okay? Is my bag in that closet?"

She headed toward the main room's coat closet. "I couldn't find it inside the one in the bedroom...."

Fuck, this was all my fault. I had to fix it.

"Hold on, Kayla, hold on!"

I rushed over and caught her by the wrist before she could make it to the empty closet where her bag most definitely was not. "Listen. Let me make this shite meal up to you. What do you want for breakfast tomorrow?"

"No. No. No." She shook her head. "You don't have to offer me breakfast just to be nice. And I should probably be getting back to my hotel anyway. Let me fetch my bag, and I'll get out of your hair."

She tried to tug her wrist away.

That only made me grip my hand even tighter around her arm.

So, not only was I holding her luggage hostage, but I also had her wrist bound, like some kind of unhinged kidnapper. Yet I couldn't bring meself to physically let her go.

"What happened earlier—we were both there, right?" I tried and failed to keep the desperate note out of my voice. "Do you really think there's any way in hell I don't want that to happen again?"

"But..." She stopped trying to get her hand back. However, her expression filled with confusion. "You were so quiet during dinner. Then you just started glaring at me because... Why, exactly, if you don't want me to go?"

Fuck me. I couldn't blame her for being puzzled by my behavior. Bloody hell, I was confused meself. Desiring someone the way I did her was a brand-new situation for me. A mind-fuck and a half.

Maybe that was why the truth came spilling out of my gob without me trying to put any kind of spin on it. "Because I was kickin' meself for takin' you so fast against the window. Because I regret not removin' your bra to get a gawp at those beautiful breasts of yours before I lost all control. Because I was fightin' the urge to rip that bulky hoodie off ya and sue the shite company that made it for defamation. Because I was holdin' meself back from sweepin' the table and takin' you again on top of it. Because I'd rather be talkin' about how to make my piss-poor performance up to you than just about anythin' else right now."

I shook my head at her. "Finish that 'because' any way you want to, Kayla. But know that it's not because I don't want you here."

I pulled her to me and shuddered at the feel of her soft body against mine. "I more than want you here. I can barely think, I want you here so bad. Feel..."

I had absolutely zero non-disclosure agreements signed, and there was a high-percentage chance that if Kayla found out who I really was, this could all blow up in my face and end in a lawsuit. Maybe a couple of them.

But I brought her hand down to the front of my jeans anyway.

"Kayla, *feel*..." I pushed her hand down past my waistband, where the beast I was trying to keep at bay resided. "Feel for yourself what you do to me."

She let out a little gasp. I thought she might snatch her hand away. Maybe even accuse me of being a pervert for making her touch me this way.

But instead, she gave it a squeeze, almost exploratory in nature. Then suddenly, I was the one taking a swift intake of breath.

My erection pulsed under her touch, threatening to release again just because she was giving it some attention. Did she have any idea, I mean, even a clue, what she did to me?

Apparently not.

"Something wet's coming out, but it's not..." Her voice scrunched up with innocent confusion. "What is that?"

Jesus Christ. This mouse...

Still, I unzipped my jeans and pulled my erection out so she could see for herself exactly what she was doing to me.

"Pre-cum. Means I'm excited. Proper excited." I battled with meself to stay still as I explained, lest she stop doing what she was doing. "You've never had a man want you so bad he starts leakin' like this when you touch him?"

She looked up at me and shook her head, her brown eyes filled with innocent wonder.

"There weren't a lot of guys before my ex," she confessed on a whisper. "And no, he never wanted me quite like this...."

I immediately knew that her ex was either a prick or incredibly stupid. Probably both.

In any case, Kayla was a fantasy come true—completely wasted on a knob like that.

I could only let meself steal short glances of her dark hand, stroking my pale flesh, for fear of coming again. And soon, even looking away wasn't enough to keep the dangerous pulse of my release at bay.

"You can keep on doin' that," I told her. "But if you do, it's gonna be more than pre-cum soon here. You'll be gettin' the real deal— my spunk all over your pretty little hand."

She looked away from me shyly then.

But her hand didn't stop stroking.

And, *fuck me*... I began to spasm inside her palm.

Her eyes. I wanted her eyes.

I dipped my head in front of hers to catch them, only to have her look to the other side. While she kept on stroking.

But no fuckin' way I was gonna let this mouse escape my gaze as she gutted me with pleasure.

I once again placed my face directly in front of hers, and this time, when she tried to turn her head, I gently grabbed her around the nape. Locking my hand with the ball of my palm against her chin so she had no choice but to let me hold her gaze in mine as I told her, "I like this. I like you."

A shy glance down since she could no longer turn her head. But then her soft brown gaze returned to mine, and she whispered, "I like you, too."

I like you, too.

My balls contracted with almost painful tightness then. I threw back my head before geysering, as promised, all over her hand.

And something else, as it turned out.

When I opened my eyes, I smiled. Not just because this sweet girl had given me the best hand job I'd ever had the pleasure of experiencing, but also because at least one of my wishes had just come true.

"Looks like I messed your hoodie," I observed without any apology whatsoever in my voice. "We better take it off."

CHAPTER 8

Kayla

"Looks like I messed your hoodie. We better take it off."

My face heated with embarrassment. I couldn't say for sure what had come over me.

One moment, I was getting up to leave, and the next, I was giving Mick the kind of hand job I never would have thought myself capable of... before now.

Before *him*.

I would have figured that super out-of-character, brazen sex act would have slowed Mick down.

But his declaration about needing to take off my hoodie turned out to be a warning.

He slammed into me like a truck, his lips colliding with mine again as he advanced forward.

Does this man even know the meaning of slow? His forceful kiss pushed me into a backward stumble until we arrived at his intended destination.

The bedroom suite.

"Wait, hold on...." He drew back from the kiss just as we reached the edge of the suite's ginormous bed. "Not makin' the same mistake I did last time."

I stared up at him, breathless and confused.

Until he started taking my clothes off. This time with slow deliberation.

The fresh hoodie I'd donned less than an hour ago went right back over my head. He tossed it aside, leaving me in nothing but my green bra—which he unhooked with a simple flick of his index finger and thumb behind my back.

"Even better than I was imaginin' at dinner." His black eyes burned over the breasts he'd exposed.

And I shuddered. Even though the suite wasn't cold, my nipples puckered under his heated gaze.

"Oh, I'm kickin' meself for not takin' me time with you."

"I have regrets about earlier, too," I admitted on a cracked breath.

His burning gaze got a little hurt until I quickly explained, "I wanted to look at you, too!"

Now it was my turn to give him a heated up-and-down look. "I mean, you're so built."

He grinned. "You think I'm mad fit, then?"

I'd watched enough British sci-fi to know that "mad fit" was the American equivalent of hot.

I answered with a wry chuckle. "Obviously, you're *mad fit*. Like, in every sense of the word."

Another devastating grin. But instead of taking off his gray t-shirt, he said, "Go on, then."

I looked to both sides. "Go on, then, what?"

"Handle your regret," he clarified. "Take me shirt off. Have yourself a proper gawp. And a feel-up, too, if you want."

His offer felt like a challenge. And I took it.... Super tentatively. But still, taking off a stranger's shirt in a hotel room felt brave. Especially for me.

Prior to this, I'd been more of the "wait covered up in bed until it was time to get it on" type.

So, I felt all sorts of wicked as I pulled Mick's shirt up and over his head to reveal a torso even more aesthetic than what I'd been picturing when I felt the way his muscles rippled underneath my fingers as he took me against the window.

The gym must have been where he lived when he wasn't at work. He was covered in lean, highly defined muscle and black tattoos.

My belly was soft and a little pooched after a day of travel and dinner. But Mick's was hard, with lines upon lines of abs clearly etched into his long torso all around it.

I understood, then, why he'd invited me to have a feel along with my gawp. Polite Kayla was gone, and Greedy Kayla couldn't keep herself from reaching out and running her fingers over his divinely muscled body.

His abs drew in with a sharp breath when I ran my hands down the sides of his torso—as if he was as affected by my touch and gaze as I was by his.

My stomach tightened with a weird mixture of surprise and pride when the patch of underwear beneath his still-unzipped jeans bulged with new life.

Was he getting hard again? Was that even possible after such a short time?

Wicked curiosity moved my fingers down the indented Y above his open waistband.

"A'right, enough of that now." He grabbed my hands before I could find out the answer to those questions for myself. "This round, it's all about you."

With a surprise heft of his Greek god biceps, he tossed me backward onto the billowy white comforter and plush pillows.

The bed was so soft. It felt like landing on a cloud. Cloud nine, with a chorus of heavenly music.

But the man standing above me was no angel.

With a quick two-handed yank, he disposed of both my zebra sweatpants and my underwear before pushing off the rest of his own clothes to reveal a bottom half that matched exactly what was going on above. And then some.

I sat up on my forearms to stare openly at the long rod of flesh between his legs.

Yep, nice Kayla had definitely left the building.

Good God, was there even a single ounce of imperfection on this man?

His eyes stayed on my uncovered chest as he kicked the rest of his clothes to the side. He studied my breasts like they were a work of art, and to my surprise, he returned to full mast right before my eyes.

His new erection pointed in the direction of my womanhood. Like an erotic arrow.

The hungry look on his face made my body tingle with anticipation as he crawled toward me.

And I remembered with extreme clarity how it had felt to have him moving inside me, filling me up so thoroughly.

Yes.... I was more than ready to go again.

But this time, he seemed to be in no hurry.

Instead of kissing me, he leaned over and sucked one of my breasts into his mouth, his tongue swirling around the areola.

Meanwhile, one of his hands reached down and cupped me below with a casualness that belied how profoundly erotic it felt to have his fingers down there while his mouth worked my breast.

My forearms soon melted underneath me, and I lowered back, fully submitting to his suckle and touch. But just as I was starting to squirm from the sensations he was giving me, he let go of my breast with a devilish grin.

"Remember that promise I made ya earlier? The one about makin' it up to you?"

I let out a breathless laugh. "Oh, I'd say you've more than done that."

"Not quite yet I haven't." He stood up on his knees and parted my thighs, running his hands down the soft and sensitive insides. His eyes then swept down to the triangle between my legs.

When I realized what he was about to do, I quickly sat back up on my arms. "Oh, you don't have to do that. I'm fine with just the breast stuff—oh!"

Before I could finish assuring him that I didn't need any special treatment, he wrapped his hands over my thighs and pulled me toward him with a rough jerk that made my forearms give out.

In an instant, I was returned to a prone position, and he was sucking the bud between my legs into his mouth like he'd sucked on my breast just moments earlier.

Only this time, his mouth suckled even harder, and his tongue laved the inside of my most intimate fold. A shock wave of concentrated pleasure zapped me so hard that my hips bucked underneath his face.

He raised his head to address me with a teasing tone. "Easy there, now. I'm only just gettin' goin'."

With those chiding words, he placed a heavy arm over my pelvis to prevent any more bucking.

Then dipped his head right back down between my legs, effectively pinning me there while his tongue assaulted me with pleasure.

For several minutes there was nothing but the sound of him sucking on my most sensitive part and his tongue lapping the insides of my wet folds.

A weird feeling came over me. Frightening and new. It felt so good. Too good. My stomach coiled and knotted, as if there was something inside of me, threatening to burst.

"Too much...." I tried to explain how I was feeling. But the frightening feeling stole all my breath.

My hands fisted the sheets, and the top half of my body rolled and twisted above Mick's restraining arm, instinctively trying to get away from the sweet pain he was inflicting on me.

"I can't take any more!" I choked out. "It feels too good—"

The orgasm split me in two before I could finish telling Mick how exquisitely he was hurting me.

This time even Mick couldn't hold me down. I arched off the bed.

Yet, he kept his mouth on me, following me into the air, delving even deeper into my core as I exploded with a different kind of pleasure—a full-body wave of sensations I'd never known before.

Before Mick.

Who plunged his tongue in and out of me, prolonging the orgasm until every nerve in my entire body was lit up with the sensation of coming.

I had never felt anything like that in my entire life. Not with Dwayne. Not with anybody.

As I floated back down to Earth, I could suddenly see so clearly how little I'd settled for in my relationship with Dwayne. Constant criticism served with scraps of affection.

And so little pleasure. Nothing that came even a little bit close to what I'd just experienced.

For the second time that day, tears sprang into my eyes without warning. And though I clamped my lips, I couldn't stop the sob that escaped.

Mick abruptly stopped.

"You a'right there?" Concern had replaced the devilish smoke in his voice.

"I'm f-fine," I answered. Right before collapsing into helpless sobs.

"Aw fuck, Kayla, I'm sorry. I didn't intend to..."

Mick's apology lashed me with guilt as my vision blurred with tears.

"No, *I'm* sorry! I'm so sorry." I curled up into a fetal position on my side and squeezed my eyes closed, willing myself with all my might to stop crying.

But the tears kept coming.

How many times had I taken care of myself while Dwayne slept after getting his?

Four years! Four years of my life wasted with a man-child who only cared about himself.

"Please stop cryin', Kayla! I can't handle it. Seriously...."

Mick sounded both distressed and angry.

I couldn't blame him. I was distressed, too—and angry... so, so angry at myself!

"I'm trying to. I'm sorry. I'm so sorry!"

But I couldn't stop, no matter how embarrassing it was to be completely losing it in the bed of a sexy, blameless man who had just given me more pleasure than I ever thought possible.

The bed depressed behind me. "C'mon, then...."

The next thing I knew, I was being pulled out of my fetal position and turned into Mick's strong arms.

He lay with me there on the overly pillowed bed, stroking the back of my head as I sobbed into his bare chest. Until finally, thankfully, I calmed down, and the tears dried up.

He continued to hold me, even after I was done crying. Though he did say, "I tell ya what—this does not make a lad feel great about his make-it-up-to-you performance."

I shook my head against his chest. "It wasn't you. I mean, actually, it was you. You made me feel good. Too good. I've never..."

I sighed, instinctually wanting to hold some stuff back.

But I'd already ruined this dude's night with my crying fit.

I owed him the full truth.

I pushed down my embarrassment to tell him, "Dwayne only ever did that for me on my birthday, and even then, he was reluctant. I thought maybe I tasted bad. I actually went to the doctor a few months ago, just to make sure I didn't have anything going on down there."

After a brief moment of consideration, Mick let out a growly sound that made his chest rumble. "Yeah, I called it right. Dwayne is a proper wanker."

"I'm not sure what a wanker is," I admitted. "But if it means 'big ol' jerk,' then yes, he was one of those—not to mention a liar. I was an idiot for staying with him as long as I did."

Several moments of silence, then Mick replied in a completely reasonable tone, "Tell ya what. I'll come to the States and visit some violence upon him. Punch to the nose, kick in the goolies, headbutt. You name it, and I'll do it to this wanker right good. But just so you know, I've been told my headbutts are particularly impressive.... Okay, why are you laughin', Kayla? I'm dead serious!"

Another soft laugh escaped before I could answer. "You want to take a trip to America just to beat up my ex and probably get arrested right after?"

"I could probably pull it off without gettin' nicked." He let out a prideful snort. "I'm good at talkin' the other guy into hittin' first. And if he hits me first, it's self-defense.... Saw that on an old episode of the American version of *Law & Order*."

Earlier, it had been tears I couldn't get a handle on, but now I couldn't control my laughter.

"I'm sorry for crying," I said when I finally got over my fit of giggles. "But thanks for making me laugh. I needed that."

"It would probably only make you laugh harder, then, if I told ya that at no point today have I actually tried to make ya laugh. Yeah, yeah, now you're laughin' harder. That's it!"

With a huff, Mick let me go.

The view from the main room of the suite was impressive, but the one in the bedroom was just as dreamy I noted when he rolled over, unblocking my view of the balcony behind him.

The Eiffel Tower's golden sparkling lights framed his sinewy body as he threw a ridiculous amount of pillows off the bed before padding over to the room's main light switch.

"Well, on that note, I'm off to kip!" He flipped off all overhead lights.

My laughter instantly subsided when darkness blanketed the room before he came back over to the bed.

Oh, no. I realized I'd totally killed the mood, and now he was going to sleep. That meant I should probably—

"We'll have another go at the universe rockin' in the mornin'."

Before I could even finish my thought about leaving, he climbed back into bed and hauled me against him, settling us into a new position—him on his back, me tucked against his right side with my head lying on his chest.

We lay there like that in the silent room—the sound of Mick's heartbeat, calm and steady, beneath my ear. A peaceful feeling stole over me, replacing all the laughter and tears.

But then he asked, "How long were you with him, then?"

"Four years," I answered after a moment of hesitation. "We were together for four years."

Several more heartbeats passed before he answered. "That's a long time."

"Yeah, I know." A fresh wave of regret washed over me. "It's a long time to go out with someone without getting married."

"Long time for any kind of relationship. Don't even have mates I held onto that many years."

"Maybe because you keep headbutting them?" I suggested with a teasing tone.

He chuckled, his chest rumbling underneath my ear. "Yeah, maybe. Coupla years ago, the boys in the big office had me do one of 'em anger management courses on account of me gettin' in too many rows with the other members of my—I mean, the other blokes at work. They said if I continued on in the direction I was goin', I'd have no decent relationships left in my professional life."

"Did the course help?" I thought of the many Suns football players who'd been forced to take a few classes after game fights or charges had been filed. Nearly all of them had gone on to rack up even more game fights, criminal charges, or both.

"Actually, it did." Mick's voice took on a thoughtful note. "Maybe it was because I wanted it to work, though. After a while, all the fightin's not so much fun anymore. Now I got mantras and such to keep me from blowin' the lid off me pot. But I still don't have many mates—at work or outside of it. Guess I got used to goin' about in the world on my own."

"I'm the exact opposite," I admitted. "I've known a few of my friends since before kindergarten, and I love the people I work with. My boss bestie, Suzie, actually went to high school with me. She was the senior president of the math club, and I was the freshman treasurer."

I softly smiled at the memory.

"Anyway, I'm a serious California girl. I was born and raised in Inglewood, and that's where the Suns' front office is, so now, I work there, too. Before I got my passport to come here, I'd never left the state—not to mention the country."

"That's nice." His voice seemed a little wistful now. "You've got roots, don't ya? Good family. Great life in L.A."

"Nice, and not nice. I'm pretty unworldly, despite living in one of the most glamorous cities on Earth."

I stroked the tangle of curls on his chest. "The Suns are a big deal in Los Angeles, and Dwayne thought he deserved the best. I'm pretty sure he cheated on me because I wasn't sexy enough and didn't dress like all the other football players' girlfriends. A lot of them are TV stars and models, you know. And I tried, but at the end of the day, I was just... well, me."

"Okay, enough of that." Mick sighed and shifted me off his chest.

I jolted out of my confessional reverie, immediately realizing my mistake.

"I'm sorry. I'm sorry," I said for, like, the umpteenth time that night. "I shouldn't keep going on and on about my ex like that. This is supposed to be a one-night stand. Not a therapy session."

"Listen, Kayla..."

Mick turned on his side to face me. But instead of pushing me away, his hands found my shoulders, and he dipped his head to look me in the eye.

"I've run into people like Dwayne before. I know the deal with 'em. The crowds build 'em up, right? Convince 'em they're better than everyone else. Just 'cos they can handle a ball, they start to think they're the soddin' king of England. But I tell you what,

Kayla, at the end of the day, it's people like 'em who're the idiots and people like you who are..."

He stopped.

But I wanted to know. "People like me who are what?"

"Never mind." He flipped back over, returning to his pillow. "Let's kip off."

"No, I want to know."

"Conversation over, Kayla." He sounded almost angry with himself as he folded his arms over his chest.

I sighed and settled in on my own side of the bed, feeling a chill pass over me now that I didn't have his body heat to keep me warm.

I sat up, and to my surprise, he sprang into a sitting position, too.

"Yer not tryin' to leave again, are ya?"

"No," I answered, a little alarmed by his tone. "I am a little cold, though."

"Yeah, and..." Mick shook his head in the dark, like he was having trouble comprehending me.

"And so, I'm getting under the covers," I answered carefully. "Which is what people do when they're cold. Especially people who aren't wearing any clothes."

A moment of silence. Then: "I'm not wearin' any clothes, either. How 'bout if I get cold without your body heat to keep me warm?"

The teasing note in his voice lifted my lips back into a smile. "I don't think you need to worry about that."

"Why not, then?" His voice rang with faux offense. "I'm just as susceptible to a middle-of-the-night chill as the next bloke. Nobody likes to wake up freezin', but it feels like you're settin' me up for that exact scenario, don't it?"

Just like that, I found myself laughing again.

"And now you're havin' another laugh at me," he grumbled. "But seriously, Kayla, what if I wake up freezin'? What then?"

I bit my lip to keep from giggling. "Then you get under the covers, just like I'm about to do."

"Or, you could..."

He beckoned me to lie back down with him.

It didn't take much convincing.

I happily rejoined him on his side of the bed and settled into the position we'd been in before.

"You know, we could *both* get under the covers," I pointed out.

"Shush now, Kayla," he answered. "Off to sleep you go."

"I mean, it's the most practical thing to do."

"Tryin' to sleep here." He drew me in even closer as he said this.

So I settled back into his arms without any further argument.

Who would have guessed that the dangerously sexy man I met on the plane that afternoon would be such an avid fan of cuddling?

Eventually, we both fell asleep. And if not for the call of my bladder, we might have stayed like that the entire night.

But after a visit to the toilet, I crept back into the suite's gorgeous front room.

71

I was happy to return to snuggling with Mick in bed—giddy about it, even. But first, I needed to grab my phone and put it on a charger before crawling back into my one-night stand's unexpectedly warm arms.

However, I froze when I found my phone lit up with a new message.

From Dwayne.

I'm sorry, baby. I'm so sorry. But it was just a publicity stunt that got out of hand. Let's not throw away 4 years over this. Please can we talk???

CHAPTER 9

Mick

FOR AS LONG AS I COULD RECALL, I'D STRUGGLED WITH sleep.

In my youth, me Dad, convinced he had the second coming of David Beckham on his hands, would insist I hit the hay before nine p.m. He claimed it was because I needed to practice before he headed off to his job as a Manchester powerline worker.

Some might have thought that considerate. By the time I reached Year 6 in primary school, though, I'd sussed out it was just an excuse.

Me heading off to my room was my parents' cue to crack open a crate of Boddingtons before engaging in a full-blown row.

"Time for bed" only meant I got to listen to their nightly shouting matches from the privacy of my bedroom.

They used to rage at each other so loud and so regular that the neighbors on both sides of our terraced house knew all the ins and outs of their various grievances with one another. Not just their son, who was supposed to be getting up early to drill his football techniques the next morning.

Yeah, unless the police showed up to tell them to shut their gobs already, it'd take me ages to drift off to sleep on the familiar sound-track of my parents threatening to off each other.

Then I'd wake up in the middle of the night to eerie quiet, which was even worse.

Had they gone through with it this time? Carried out their threats to do each other bodily harm? Or worse?

My heart would race, and eventually, I'd have to venture down-stairs to make sure they hadn't really up and done what they were always saying they were gonna at the top of their lungs.

They hadn't.

I'd find them both passed out on the couch, like boxers after a knockout fight, reeking of beer and sometimes piss.

After that, there was nothing left to do but shuffle back to my room, feeling like a right proper idiot.

It would take another eon to fall back to sleep with that "completely stupid" feeling swirling around my chest—only to be kicked awake a coupla hours later by Dad calling me a lazy twat for not being dressed in my trainers and ready to go at five am sharp, like he'd told me to be.

Me dad could be a right bastard when he had a hangover. And he always had a hangover during those early morning practices.

"Think yer going to make it into the starting line-up for Manchester United with that attitude, ya fuckin' barm cake?"

He'd sneer shite like that at me if I didn't kick the ball exactly where he pointed.

But by the time I entered secondary, I already knew I wasn't going to make it into the starting line-up of his favorite team.

I intentionally chose to sign on with the Youth Training Scheme for FC Greenwich—the club Dad despised the most. I liked that it was down in London. Too far to commute on the daily. That meant at the age of seventeen, I got to leave home and, most importantly, my shite parents behind.

Turned out, though, that I'd left North Manchester behind but still hadn't escaped the crappy sleep.

Initially, it was the life of a young footballer that kept me tossing and turning. Game-day anxiety and nonstop partying, whenever we got a break, wasn't exactly a sterling recipe for the eight hours plus that the team doc recommended at my first physical.

By my late twenties, I'd gotten sick of the parties and the endless stream of women willing to go off with me just to brag they'd slept with a pro footballer.

But, all of a sudden, I began jolting awake in the middle of the night with an unexplainable ache in my chest.

I'd find meself lying there in the dark of my multi-million-dollar townhouse, wondering why I even bothered with all of that rubbish. My career, my cars, my properties... What did any of it matter when I was waking up alone in the middle of the night?

I think that might have been when my temper really started to get away from me.

I'd been a right proper bastard from the start of my career. "Nasty Andy," "Red Card Drew," "The A.M. Volcano," and "Vinnie Jones: The Sequel" were just a few of the names the British press started calling me after I gained a reputation for aggressive gameplay and on-field altercations.

Me Dad had put a massive chip on my shoulder, and I was making sure every player I encountered had to deal with it. Didn't matter whether they were on my team or not. And somewhere along the way, I started getting angry over shite that had nothing to do with what was taking place on the pitch.

I'd seethe with jealousy toward the blokes who'd married their secondary school sweethearts. The ones with parents they didn't hate. The ones who didn't have to go home to an empty property in Mayfair or some corporate sponsor hotel room on the road every night.

The truth was that more than a decade after escaping my parents' house, I still yearned for the same thing I'd wanted when I'd lived with them in North Manchester—a normal life, a normal family.

But normal girls didn't exactly run in my circles.

And the few ones I'd manage to encounter seemed more interested in the flash time I could give them than settling down into a nice, quiet life with a rough footballer.

So, yeah, sleep continued to be something I struggled with—until I invited an American who had no clue who I was into my bed.

That night, I fell asleep with Kayla in my arms. Easily. Without even having to pop one of the pills the football club's doctor had prescribed me.

And this sleep was way better than the usual drug-induced blackness. Peaceful, deep, and filled with dreams of my sexy American riding on top of me, her hips undulating as I played with her heavy breasts.

So, no, I wasn't surprised to wake up the next morning to find my manhood at full stand. But I was surprised to find my arms empty.

My heart seized, and I immediately rolled my head to see if she'd migrated to the other side of the bed during the night—maybe gotten under the covers like she'd been threatening to do before we fell asleep.

Fuck me, though. There was nothing but white bed linens and the few pillows I hadn't thrown to the ground last night.

Kayla, the woman who had been responsible for my first non-drug-induced good night of sleep ever, was gone. Just gone.

Or maybe...

I quickly sat up to direct my hopeful gaze toward the open door of the WC, where she'd left her smaller rolling suitcase last night.

But, yeah, that bag was gone, too.

I cursed. She'd done a runner, then. And I couldn't even blame her.

All that pillow talk last night...

Me confessing my fight history and Johnny-no-mates status before I insisted on snuggling with her—y'know, right after I refused to let her get under the covers.

Yeah, I'd come off like a proper nutter, hadn't I?

Good job, Atwater, me Dad sneered inside my head.

Was it any wonder she'd run off the first chance she—

The bedroom door suddenly flew open, interrupting my self-pity fest.

"Oh, yay, you're up! Sorry for the door bang. My hands are totally full...."

All of a sudden, Kayla was noisily entering the room with a cardboard cup holder filled with two coffees in one hand and a bag with the name of a pâtisserie written on it in refined blue letters in the other.

I blinked at her, my heart draining the fear and refilling with relief. "I thought you'd done a runner."

"Oh, yeah, I can see how you'd think that. I totally should have left you a note." She guiltily shifted her eyes away from mine. "But I was afraid they'd cancel my hotel reservation, so I dashed over there with my bag to check in super-early this morning. Then I got us some croissants on the way back—or I guess I'm supposed to say *croissant.*"

She set the bag and the coffees down on the dresser underneath the flatscreen TV with a little laugh. "Anyway, it took forever to find coffee because every place I went acted like they didn't even understand the concept of a to-go cup. *Then* there were these two guys with cameras outside the front entrance of your hotel's lobby."

She shook her head and tore the tops off two sugar packets. "They were asking me all these questions in French? Only thing I understood was 'What's your name?' And that's only because it's all over my French phrasebook."

My chest froze. Paparazzi. She was talking about a couple of paparazzi, hanging around outside the hotel. Possibly even following up on the mystery woman plane story.

"What did you say to 'em?" I asked her with my heart in my throat.

"Well, of course, I told them my name was Kasha—like, from sasha x kasha, that American sister singing act?" She grinned as she poured the sugar into one of the cups of coffee. "I mean, they just assumed I had to be famous. Why? Because I'm a Black woman walking into the front entrance of an expensive hotel?"

Another wave of relief crashed through me, sagging my chest. I was almost grateful to American racism for skewing Kayla's automatic assumptions about the sudden interest from the French press.

"Maybe next time you leave, you should go through the garage entrance," I suggested. "The French butler told me earlier that's what all the celebs do."

"The real celebs?" She threw me a cheeky grin. "Not just the ones claiming they're Beyoncé?"

I couldn't help but smile back, albeit rather weakly. "Fake famous people can use that entrance, too. 'Cording to the butler, a lot of paparazzi hang 'round this place, so sometimes it's the only way to avoid 'em."

"I'll keep that in mind." She replaced the lid on her takeout cup before finally turning back to look at me. "By the way, what do you take in your cof—oh, well... um..."

Her full lips formed into an "O" of surprise when she saw the state of me below the waist. "I'm sorry.... I didn't realize..."

She looked away, embarrassed, but I just grinned and decided to finish the sentence for her. "You didn't realize you'd be greeted by another kind of Eiffel Tower when you returned to my hotel room?"

"No, um, I didn't... Do you...?"

She continued to openly stare at my self-dubbed Eiffel Tower.

"Do you... um... need help with that?"

My little mouse was learning to be brave. A strange kind of pride washed over me on her behalf.

"Know what?" I answered. "I'll take any help you're willin' to give a bloke in need."

"Okay, um, I've got this! I think...." Kayla set down her coffee and shimmied out of her winter coat.

She'd bought another sweatshirt to replace the one I spunked on, I noted. This one had *J'aime Paris* written across it, and there was an Eiffel Tower where the A in Paris would normally be.

But perhaps she remembered what happened to her last clean shirt because she quickly pulled the new hoodie off, revealing a pink bra with cherry-red piping around its edges. Next came her zebra sweats, which uncovered a matching pair of pink bikini briefs with cherry-red trim.

It made me truly wonder why all the other birds I'd hooked up with chose lace over cotton underthings. The cherry-and-pink ensemble displayed her heavily rounded breasts and ample backside perfectly. Like a dessert.

A dessert I wanted to lick all over.

But I made meself lean back on my forearms and wait for her to come to me.

I wanted to see what she'd do next—slightly more than I desired to take her out of her enticing underthings.

Padding over to stand beside the bed, she studied my straining erection. As if it was one of her math club problems in need of solving.

"I could..." She took me in her hand and worked me up and down a few times—only to quickly release me, like she'd been caught doing something wrong. "No, I already did that."

Truth was, I wouldn't have minded another go inside her palm. My body had thrilled at her touch, then ached when she'd stopped.

But any regrets I had about missing out on a second handie disappeared almost as soon as she crawled onto the bed and positioned herself between my legs.

I drew in my breath with a sharp hiss when she took me in her mouth. Forgot all about that hand shandy she cut short! Bolts of red-hot pleasure pulsed through my shaft as she worked her lips down it.

Usually, this was the bit where I closed my eyes and just enjoy being attended to by whoever was down there.

But I couldn't look away from Kayla framed in the morning light —her gorgeous bottom up in the air, her gaze locked into mine while her head bobbed up and down on my manhood.

I was completely mesmerized by the delicious picture she was presenting. Just for me.

"Christ, Kayla..." I reached down to grasp the back of her head, guiding her into a nice rhythm.

And that was a mistake.

It soon became too much, and I had to pull out of her mouth with a curse.

"Did I do something wrong?" Kayla blinked up at me, clearly distressed.

"Nah, I just..." I reached into the nightstand and grabbed a condom. I was so close. It was a wonder I didn't come in my own bloody hand before getting it on.

But the promise of what was awaiting me if I held on to my load got me through.

"Time to make a dream come true."

I waggled my eyebrows at Kayla before hauling her into a kneeling position over the erection I could barely contain.

Pulling the crotch of her pink underwear aside with one hand, I guided her hips down with the other. Our combined moan filled the room when I sat her down on my erection.

Then I unhooked her bra, tossed it aside, and we were off to the races.

I leaned back, and Kayla let out a sweet groan as she began moving on top of me while I started pistoning into her from below.

After that, all I had to do was reach up to make the rest of my dream come true. I massaged her glorious breasts in my large hands as the slap of our bodies joining together became the only sound in the room.

This was just like the dream. Better, actually.

We moved in synchronous motion, Kayla leaned forward with her hands grasped over mine as she met my every thrust with a roll of her sweet hips.

I was a lion. And she was a mouse. But we were magic together as we sought out an unnamable thing in each other.

We were perfect. Just perfect.

Up to and including when we came at the same time. Her with a happy cry, and me with an urgent groan. Both my hands fell to her waist, pulling her hips tight into mine.

Only then did I close my eyes, convulsing into her and shuddering to a conclusion with my hands viced around her soft, beautiful body.

"Did that help with your Eiffel Tower problem?"

She laughed after collapsing onto my chest in a happy heap.

She was joking. But the joke was on her, wadn't it? I could already feel meself growing harder inside her. "Gotta feelin' I'm going to be needin' your help again in a few more minutes."

"Tribute!" she volunteered.

Even I'd read just enough to know that was a *Hunger Games* joke.

But then she composed her face to regard me with a stern look. "Listen, I'm totally willing to help you, but first you've got to give me back my big suitcase. Seriously, I had to buy this hoodie this morning, and now I'm all out of underwear!"

Christ, this woman was somehow even cuter and sexier when she pouted.

"We'll see..." I let out an evil chuckle and flipped us over so that I was back on top. "First, you've gotta earn it..."

CHAPTER 10

Kayla

Apparently, I did an adequate job during our second round of morning sex.

Not only did Mick (ignoring my many protests) order breakfast from room service after the croissants I'd bought got cold, but he also finally had my big suitcase brought up to the suite.

However, the suitcase was currently still sitting outside the bathroom's open door.

Lonely and unopened.

And I was currently feeling the exact opposite of that.

I mean, I was extremely happy and all the way cracked open after two rounds of morning sex.

Also, ridiculously languid as I lounged in the opulent bathroom's claw-foot tub, propped up against Mick's chest.

Yes, I, Kayla "so, so boring" Edwards, was enjoying the prettiest-smelling bath I'd ever taken while being hand-fed strawberries by the most engaging man I'd ever met.

I was pretty sure I wasn't dreaming. I'd already pinched myself a few times this morning—so had Mick!

But still...

"I'm going to have to try super-hard not to get used to this," I reminded myself out loud as I reached toward the room service tray that Mick had set up on a stool beside the tub.

I tried to grab a square of chocolate wrapped in shiny gold foil.

Only to have Mick slap it out of my hand and demand, "What you gettin' up to, then?"

"I was just going to unwrap one of these chocolates," I answered defensively. "You know, because I'm totally capable of feeding myself?"

"See, that's why you'd be better off lettin' me do the heavy liftin' when it comes to this breakfast business."

He nudged me forward and sat up fully in the tub behind me. "Here's how you do up chocolate real proper-like in a continental breakfast...."

His voice took on the tone of a schoolteacher as he tore off a third of one of the croissants and buttered it. Then he deftly unwrapped the piece of chocolate I'd tried to pick up a few moments ago.

"First, you take your buttered bread, open it up, pop this bit of chocolate in between, like so, and voilà, mate, ya got the finest breakfast this side of the Atlantic!"

I bit into the piece of croissant he put up to my lips, and my taste buds reeled. "Oh, my freaking gosh! The butter and chocolate melting together in my mouth tastes so good. I can't believe we don't eat them this way in America."

"Lots of things hard to believe 'bout the States." Mick turned to butter and added another square of chocolate to the rest of the croissant. "You don't like our kind of football over there, either. How's that?"

"Well, let's see...." I pretended to give his question serious consideration. "American football is interesting and exciting, with really funny commercials in between. While your kind of football is... How can I put this nicely? Like, *really freaking* boring. Even the cute guys running around in short shorts aren't enough to make up for the lack of action in the game. I mean, there's barely any scoring!"

I felt him go still behind me. "Have you never heard the term *football is life*, then?"

"Life, like one of those *life sentences*?" I asked innocently. "The ones where your captor tortures you with boredom until you lose all will to live?"

"Take that back!"

"Where is the lie?" I demanded, standing my ground like a hot-take American Revolutionary.

Mick growled. "Take it back, Kayla, or you're gonna get it."

"Oh, my God." I made my voice breathless with fear. "Are you going to make me watch soccer? Please don't do that, Mick! It would be too cruel! The extreme punishment does not fit the crime!"

"Okay, that's it."

Mick reached out and grabbed me.

And no, he didn't make me watch a boring game of soccer. But he did tickle me mercilessly until I screamed, "I'm sorry! I'm sorry! Okay, okay, I take it all back!"

However, by the time I gave in, something else had joined us in the tub.

"Surrender's no longer enough," Mick murmured into my ear above his resurrected Eiffel Tower.

He reached for what turned out to be an auspiciously placed condom and informed me, "You did the crime! Now you'll have to serve the time!"

Okay, did I say we had two rounds of morning sex? Make that three.

Mick took me from behind, sloshing water over the sides of the tub with the force of his punishing strokes.

"Now it's my turn to apologize." He settled me back onto his chest with a tired laugh after we'd both come a third time. "Can't seem to keep my hands off you, can I? Jesus Christ, look at the mess we made."

Yes, look at this mess. My heart stuttered, a sinking sensation replacing the cracked, wide-open one from before.

Mick had given me not one, not two—but *three* orgasms.

Yet, I'd failed to tell him the truth when I came back to the hotel room.

"I lied to you!" I confessed with a rush of breath, unable to hold it in anymore.

Mick stiffened behind me. "What?"

"I lied to you earlier when I said I left to go check into my hotel. I mean, I did check into my room at the Benton Budget. But I didn't decide to do that until I woke up to a text. A text from Dwayne."

Mick didn't speak right away. I could swear the temperature of the bathwater actually dropped a few degrees by the time he finally responded.

"So that wanker came to his senses and begged you to take him back."

I jolted. "How did you know?"

"Look at you, Kayla." I sensed Mick shake his head behind me. "What bloke in his right mind would choose some reality barm cake over you?"

His tone implied that his reasoning was obvious. But I had to point out, "Lots of men would choose a reality star over me. Especially in L.A."

"Then lots of blokes in L.A. are stupid." Mick's voice took on a note of finality. Like a king making the kind of decree you weren't allowed to argue against.

My heart did all sorts of gymnastics in my chest.

I didn't know whether to feel supremely complimented or utterly guilty.

So I just pressed on with my confession. "Anyway, his text brought up a lot of feelings. And that's why I left—why I really left. I should have told you as soon as I returned to the room. But I didn't. And I'm really, really sorry about that."

A long, tense beat.

And when Mick spoke again, his voice was quieter but somehow harder at the same time. "So, you only returned here to get your luggage before swingin' like a pendulum back to your wanker ex? The sex was—what then? Some kinda consolation prize for your sad one-night stand?"

"Wait. That's where you think I'm going with this confession?" I sat up and turned around to look at him—at least as much as I could, considering the tub's tight confines.

"I left because I didn't think it was fair to answer Dwayne's text while you were asleep in the next room. But even after I checked into my hotel room, it still didn't feel right to answer him. Like, it was just crystal clear that Dwayne didn't deserve even a second more of my attention. So, I blocked him instead."

I let out a long breath. "I blocked him. Then I came right back here. To get my luggage—but also to have breakfast with you. Like I *promised*. Mick, I'm so sorry I confused you with my behavior."

I laid a hand over my heart. "I get that this is just a one-night stand, but I wanted to be honest with you. Because, at least for today, you're the one who deserves my attention right now. Not him."

"Honest..." Mick stared back at me, his black eyes cagey and assessing. Then he asked, "You really hate our kind of football that much?"

I furrowed my brow, jolting at the sudden callback to our totally silly conversation from earlier. "I mean, hate is a strong word. *Meh* is probably a better descriptor."

I laughed a little, but Mick's expression remained serious, bordering on grave. "So, if a big footballer came along, someone with real flash and enough money to stay at this place without Tourmaline having to put up the dosh—the kind of footballer 'em paps outside would be gaggin' to get a picture of. If one of 'em had also put it to you on that plane, you're sayin' you'd be like, 'Thanks for the offer, mate, but I'd rather hook up with this nobody electrician I just met. Toodle-oo!'?"

I squinted, not completely sure I understood the question. "Are you asking me if I'd rather get with a famous soccer player than with you?"

"Yeah." Mick gritted his jaw. "Somethin' like that."

"No!" My answer came out in an instant, without a second of thought. "First of all, I don't ever want to get with any kind of pro athlete ever again. Football, baseball, soccer, I don't care. As far as I can tell, even the players who seem nice are liars and cheats. And second of all..."

My face heated, despite the now lukewarm bath water. "I don't want to sound too thirsty, but I like you. And it's not just about the sex. I think you're kind and smart and funny—even if you're not trying to be that last one.

Too much! Too much! I knew I was being all sorts of extra, considering that this was only supposed to be a one-night stand.

But I pressed on with my confession. "I mean, you're a really great and down-to-earth guy. I'd rather watch you fix a downed electric power line than watch any kind of sports star play whatever he plays, any day of the week."

Mick just stared at me with an unreadable expression on his face.

I'd meant to reassure him.

But instead of breathing easy, he abruptly set me forward and away from him. Then he climbed out of the tub in a cascade of water and flexing muscles.

Oh God, had I gone too far? Completely messed this up?

"Mick?" I asked, kicking myself.

He just snatched a towel from the warming rack without looking at me.

Suddenly, I missed his weirdly intense eyes. A cold chill ratcheted through me as I watched him dry off his Greek god body, and I miserably noted that he no longer sported even the hint of an erection.

"Best ya climb out of that bath now and get yerself dressed." Mick threw the large towel down on top of the puddle we'd made. "I'll meet you back in the main room. Got somethin' I need to tell ya. And it's best we have this conversation with our clothes on."

CHAPTER 11

Mick

CHRIST, WHAT HAVE I GONE AND DONE?

After slipping on a tracksuit over some sweat-wicking thermal base layers, I headed out to the main suite and began just pacing back and forth while I waited to break the news to Kayla about who I truly was.

In the beginning, it all felt like a bit of a game, dinnit? She was vibing on me, as the Americans say, and I was right into her, too. Baggage had to be nicked and quite a few things about meself omitted in order to make our one-nighter happen.

Misleading her about who I was had seemed like the obvious solution to get what we both wanted. At first.

But what she'd said in the bath...

All that stuff about liking the bloke I was pretending to be more than a flash footballer? It had me head in a proper spin, dinnit?

On one side, it swelled my heart to massive proportions to hear she'd choose the guy I was pretending to be over some hypothetical big-name football player.

On the other hand, I was, in fact, a big-name football player.

And she'd made it clear as day she didn't want nothing to do with the real me.

Though, that was the actual problem, whadn't?

I felt like the real me when I was with her. The one I'd been hiding since I moved out of North Manchester. With her, I was a regular bloke, not wound up over nothing all the time—almost easygoing.

She brought out the man I'd always wanted to be. A bloke worthy of the time and attention of a great woman like her.

But now I had to tell her....

I wasn't an electrician in real life. Nope. I was one of them pro athletes she couldn't stand.

How would a chat like that even go?

So yeah, I was pacing and muttering all sorts of cuss words when the phone I'd left charging face down on top of the wet bar started vibrating.

Then I cussed even louder when I picked it up and saw the time.

The Tourmaline was one of them hotels that made you think time didn't matter when you were inside their luxury confines. There weren't any obvious clocks anywhere. Not even on the nightstand.

So, when I picked up the phone, I discovered it wasn't "maybe around 8ish" like I'd thought when I decided to run Kayla and me that bath.

More like after 11 am. I was supposed to be at the Paris Triomphe closed practice over an hour ago!

I'd totally lost track of time during my morning activities with Kayla, and now it was verging on afternoon.

And underneath that, later than expected, at 11:12, sat a veritable wall of missed call notifications and text messages from my manager/agent, Gerald.

"HEY MICK-O, WHERE ARE YOU? WHY AREN'T YOU answering your phone? The car the club sent for you is waiting downstairs."

THE FIRST FEW MESSAGES GERALD SENT A BIT AFTER 9 am started out polite. But the ones he sent through after 10 am were screaming in all caps.

"WHY DID YOU TELL THE FRONT DESK NOT TO LET ANY CALLS THROUGH???!! THE CAR'S BEEN WAITING FOR HOURS!!! WHERE THE HELL ARE YOU??? ARE YOU TRYING TO RUIN EVERYTHING WE PLANNED???!!!

BLOODY HELL. I RUBBED A HAND OVER MY FACE.

Gerald was cheesed off—and I could only imagine how the team we wanted to make me an eight-figure leverage offer must be feeling right now.

But I couldn't head downstairs to meet the car until I sorted things out with Kayla. I owed her at least that much.

I was typing Gerald back that I was gonna be at least fifteen more minutes when Kayla came out of the bedroom, pulling her big suitcase behind her.

"Give me a tick," I said, lifting a finger her way.

"No need. I'll just see myself out."

Instead of stopping in front of me and sweetly waiting for me to finish up my text to Gerald, Kayla kept walking right on past me. Toward the suite's front door!

"Whoa, hang on a minute!"

I chucked down the phone without finishing the text and swiftly moved in front of her, blocking her path. "Where do ya think you're goin'? We're meant to have a chat!"

She pulled up short, looking truly puzzled. As if she was genuinely surprised by me trying to stop her from leaving. "No, we totally don't have to have a chat. I get it, Mick."

She raised her eyes to the ceiling and shook her head. "I said too much. And I confused you. And I totally creeped you out. You don't have to tell me all of that. I'm sorry, okay? I'm sorry for acting like such a psycho. This is why I can't have nice things. So, I'm just going to leave—no conversation required."

"Hold on, you think you're the one actin' like a nutter in this scenario?"

It took all of my self-control not to laugh in her face. She truly didn't have a clue, did she?

"No, that would be me," I assured her. "Here's the thing, Kayla...."

I opened my mouth to tell her the truth I'd been holding back since we met on the plane.

But nothing came out.

Nothing but a voice in my head practically shouting, *No! You can't tell her. It'll ruin everything. She'll never speak to you again!*

I tamped down the loud voice and tried again. "Here's what I need to tell you...."

No, don't do it! the voice roared before I could finish. Even louder than before. *She's already halfway out the door with her suitcase packed. What the bloody hell do you think she'll do when you tell her you're a football star? Fuck, are you mental?*

"Yes, I am mental! Obviously!"

I didn't realize I'd answered the voice out loud until Kayla shook her head and wearily insisted, "No, you're not, Mick. And I appreciate you trying to be so nice about me oversharing. Truly, I appreciate everything you did for me yesterday and this morning. But I really should go and let you get on with your own life now."

With that, she swerved to the left and went around me to resume her march toward the exit.

And I almost let her go.

The thing was, I'd never been a coward. I'd told some of the biggest football players in the world exactly what was on my mind before knocking them in their teeth. But this much smaller American was proving more than I could handle.

It occurred to me that allowing her to walk out that door might be the best solution for everyone involved.

For a moment, I imagined just letting her leave with the impression that she was the one in the wrong and had simply gotten too close.

Seriously, how many other birds had I escorted to hotel doors just for insinuating they wanted to see me again and maybe go on a "real date"?

"Real Date" Translation: Use you to be seen out with a famous footballer in a posh restaurant and make my friends jealous.

If I let Kayla walk out the door now without telling her who I was, she'd get on with her trip, and I'd get on with mine.

She'd return to the States none the wiser and probably never figure out that her one-night stand in Paris had really been a world-famous footballer.

I considered that scenario. Considered just letting it happen.

Then, I used all my athletic training to sprint backward and hard shift to the left to block her path again.

"Seriously, where are you goin'?" I demanded, like the much bigger-than-her nutter she hadn't quite sussed out I truly was yet.

She pulled up short again, her brow furrowing. "Um, back to my hotel? I'm getting out of your hair. Like I said."

A truth spilled out then. But it wasn't the one I'd been intending to tell her while I was pacing back and forth.

"I don't want you to go back to your hotel!"

She blinked at me. Several times. Then she jutted her chin forward to ask, "If you don't want me to go, then why did you get out of the bath like that? Tell me we need to have a talk with our clothes on?"

My Adam's apple bobbed as I swallowed down the whole truth—then came back with a partial lie. "Listen, I'm supposed to be at the Parc des Rois Stadium right now, attendin' a closed practice for the Paris Triomphe football club. It's, ah... somethin' to do with the prize package, and they've actually got a car waitin' for me downstairs in the garage."

Her eyes widened. "Oh, my gosh, that's why you were asking me all that stuff about soccer? And why you were suddenly in such a rush to get out of the bath? Why didn't you say something earlier?"

I went with another partial truth to answer her last question. "I didn't say anythin' because I can't take ya with me, and I was enjoyin' me morning with you. I didn't want it to end. And, I know you don't consider us a proper swipe-right scenario, but..."

I waggled both my hands between us, just like she did the night before. "I don't want this to end. I don't want us to end. Not yet."

She stared at me for a few moments, her pretty brown eyes filled with shock.

But then her expression softened, and she admitted, "I don't want us to end, either!"

"A'right, then." I didn't realize I'd been holding my breath until it rushed out of me in one relieved burst. "Neither of us want this to end. Cheers to that. Tell you what, Kayla."

I reached around her and took the big suitcase from her, like it was a kid in a hostage negotiation.

"Instead of leavin' with this one, why don't you go to that Benton Budget and get your other suitcase and bring it back here...."

"Bring it back here?" She shook her head. "Why?"

"Cos you never shoulda taken it outta here in the first place."

I guess I was done pretending to be any form of low-key with her. I pulled her to me like I'd been wanting to do ever since she came out of the bedroom, fully reclothed in that fuck-awful purple hoodie.

"Kayla, listen to me. I ain't tryin' to get rid of you." I gently grasped her around the back of her neck with both hands and stroked my thumbs over her soft jawline. "I'm askin' you to stay with me for the rest of my holiday."

She made an uncertain humming sound and glanced to the side.

"But, Mick, this is crazy. We only just met. Less than twenty-four hours ago."

"Yeah, told you I was way more mental than you, didn't I?" I let out a wry laugh.

But then, I got serious again.

"That's why we have to make the rest of my time here count."

I rested my forehead against hers. "Stay here with me, at least until my three days in Paris are done? Will ya do that?"

"Mick..."

She shook her head against mine.

And for perhaps the last time ever, I pleaded, "Don't say no, Kayla."

CHAPTER 12

Mick

Done banging your American yet? In town. Wanna meet up for drinks at my new club?

MY HEART SANK WHEN I READ THE MESSAGE FROM MAX. When I opened the temporary locker Triomphe gave me to find my phone lit with a just-left message, I'd been hoping to find a text from Kayla.

I'd given her the digits to my personal line this morning after she said yes to staying on in the penthouse with me.

But no, it was just Max, who'd apparently had so little to do in his over-indulgent life he'd cut his Mykonos trip short to come to Paris to possibly hang with me.

Any other time, I'd take him up on this offer. Max was the last holdover from my hard-partying days. The kind of bloke who'd invite you to a barn rave on the outskirts of Berlin one night, then fly you to a whiskey library he'd been meaning to try in Japan the next night.

Truth was, he didn't even need me to have a good time anywhere in the world. He'd told me point-blank at one of those whiskey bars he liked so much that he only hung on to me because I reminded him of his older brother. "Except you don't hate my guts. Guess our relationship's kind of like the therapy my nan keeps on insisting I need."

Still, he'd been right about him being the only reason I ever took any kind of real vacation. And I didn't love adding more guilt to the dumpster fire of it already burning in my stomach as I typed back.

SORRY, MATE...

I HESITATED. ON ONE SIDE, I FELT LIKE I OWED HIM A good excuse for why I couldn't make it out to his club. On the other hand, I didn't like the idea of continuing to pass Kayla off as some bird I was just using for a cover story.

Obviously, she was more than that at this point.

My mind spirited back to earlier in the day, when I'd kissed her goodbye for so long that she gently pushed me away, reminding me, "You have to go!"

Yeah, I did. But even with an eight-figure deal on the line, I could barely tear meself away.

"I'll be gone for at least five hours, so do whatever ya want today," I'd told her. "But when I get back, I want you here with your other bag. You understand?"

She nodded in the sweet, shy way I couldn't get enough of. "I understand. I think both of us are being a little crazy. But I understand. And I'll come here with my little bag. I promise."

"Good girl. C'mere..." I pulled her back into my arms to award her dutiful answer and kissed her again. And again. Then one more time before I made meself back away from her with my hands raised in the air.

"Enough of that, woman! If I let meself kiss ya one more time, you'll be on your back, and I'll be later than I already am."

"I'm not one keeping you here!" Kayla answered with a giggle.

I threw her a censorious look. "Well, you know that's a lie, don't ya? You're a veritable sinkhole of temptation!"

Then I asked her, "Why're you laughin' *again*? I have yet to make a joke."

Kayla's sweet laughter echoed in my ears, filling me with even more guilt as I finished up my text to Max with some vague excuse about hanging out with the team tonight.

Max immediately replied.

> **Come through, my guy! VIP's big enough for everyone, and you know the owner.**

Should have guessed Max would respond with the rich bro equivalent of "the more the merrier."

I grimaced, trying to figure out how to respond.

"Hello. Atwater, yes?" a voice said on the other side of the locker door before I could come up with a reply for Max. "Coach Ollie is asking for you to join him and Monsieur Zaman upstairs before the last session of practice."

I turned to find the Triomphe's winger captain, Bruno Monceaux, grinning at me like whatever they called the French version of a Labrador retriever.

I frowned, thinking about how Coach Ollie had rushed away after blowing the whistle after the first portion of practice. At least, it was the first for me. It was second to last for everybody else.

Bloody hell, he must have gone straight up to the owner's office to tell him how shite I played at the practice they'd closed just for me. Might be they'd already decided against making me an offer.

"Should I not call you Atwater?" Bruno's face fell, mistaking the reason for my scowl. "Is there some other name you prefer?"

"Nah, mate, you're a'right," I answered. "I narrowly slipped out of one tough conversation today. I reckon it figures the football gods had to give me a makeup."

"What? I'm sorry, I don't understand."

Neither would Gerald when I called to explain to him how I'd blown an expected eight-figure offer because I'd been distracted by an American woman I met yesterday.

But to Bruno, I said, "Just show me the way, I guess."

"Thank you so much for joining us for the afternoon's portion of our practice," Bruno said as he led me out of the locker room and down an industrial grey hall. "I had my doubts when you came so late. But I could not believe how generous you were on the field! I was very honored by the many times you passed me the ball to me instead of making the goal yourself."

Apparently, Bruno was not nearly as unimpressed with my performance as Coach Ollie. But that so-called "generous" play was probably most of the reason why Zahir Zaman, the crazy-rich new owner of the Triomphe football club, had summoned me to his office to yank his offer.

I'd been so distracted by thoughts of Kayla that I'd barely paid attention at practice. Instead of my usual aggressive gameplay, I'd played the game on autopilot, kicking the ball to whoever was in the best position instead of always going for it on my own.

Coach Ollie had asked for the Atomic Foot, and I'd given them Mr. Nice Guy.

Zoning out had been a big mistake. One I'd have to pay for in millions of euros.

"I sense you are here with me now. But perhaps your mind is somewhere else, yes?" Bruno's voice cut short my spiraling thoughts. "Is there something you would like to talk with me about? I am told I have very good listening ears. In fact, this is why I was voted in as team captain after Coach Ollie's arrival."

I squinted at him. "You were voted in? Coach Ollie didn't just appoint you?"

"*Non! Non! Non!*" Bruno answered with a wry smile. "When Coach Ollie comes to our club, he says he desires to do things differently from FC Greenwich. We vote on everything, you should know, including offering you a closed practice opportunity."

"Hold on." I furrowed my brow like Kayla did when I got in front of her to stop her from leaving. "You actually voted on whether to offer me the opportunity to try out for a multi-million euro contract?"

"*Oui*, this our way!" Bruno replied with a proud nod. "And I will not lie to you, Atwater, the vote was very close. We liked the idea of taking on a midfielder with such a powerful yet precise kick as yours. But we feared you might not fit in with our team culture."

I could only shake my head at this new information. "You're right, then. Triomphe's not a thing like FC Greenwich."

FC Greenwich Youth Training Camp had been more like a Spartan gladiator-type culling cycle than a true opportunity. Players were pitted against each other.

If any of the coaches so much as sniffed a friendship in the offing, they'd made sure to place those two lads in sudden-death matches. That what they called it when the final score decided who would be coming back to practice the next day and who would be sent home to wherever in England they came from before they showed up on the Greenwich field stadium pitch with their pro-footballer dreams.

I knew from the start that I wasn't going back to North Manchester.

So, I'd done whatever it took to make sure I stayed on with the Youth Club, while the other boys in my sudden-death matches got sent home in tears.

By the time I made it into the official starting lineup for FC Greenwich, I'd learned the lesson Greenwich tried to teach all of its players as early as possible. Everybody was competition. Even your teammates.

Ned, the captain of FC Greenwich, had been a plant more than anything. Narked to the coach about any injuries players might be trying to hide, and especially any fights that broke out in the locker room.

I'd gotten narked on a lot. Hence the anger management course.

But here was Bruno, offering to do something that wouldn't have ever occurred to Ned the Narc.

Listen.

"Does this distraction of yours have something to do with the woman you are being linked to on PureFootball.com?" Bruno asked, his voice gentle with understanding.

I glowered as we walked up a set of stairs.

"PureFootball is a gossip site," Bruno explained, once again mistaking the reason for my angry look. "Perhaps you have never heard of it somehow?"

"I sussed what it is," I snapped before he could finish his careful explanation. "Just don't like the idea of her being on some waste gossip site."

Bruno nodded sagely. "I see. You are really forming the heart connection with this woman. It is the romance, not only the sex. I am assuming she is the true reason you missed the first part of our morning practice. And I am guessing she is the one you think of even now as we go to speak with Coach Ollie and Monsieur Zaman. Perhaps it is not a holiday fling, as PureFootball suspects? Perhaps you really like her?"

"Yeah," I admitted against my better judgment. "It's a long story, but yeah, I genuinely like her."

"Oh, I like long stories," Bruno assured me. "I read Victor Hugo's *Les Misérables* when I was twelve. Two times. But alas, we are here."

Bruno came to a stop in front of a closed door.

"Tell you what. I will wait out here to hear your long story!" he offered.

Then he knocked on the door before giving me a chance to answer.

"Come in!" Coach Ollie called out from the other side of the door.

And I put back on my game face as I walked in to face the firing squad.

Hold on. What the...?

My footsteps stuttered a bit.

Coach Ollie was standing beside a desk, behind which sat Zahir Zaman, the CEO of the Tourmaline Group. That, I was expecting.

But I wasn't prepared for the two gorgeous Black women sitting on the couch closest to Zaman's desk.

They appeared identical in every way. From the top of their waist-length silky hair extensions to the hemlines of their knee-length but body-hugging sweater dresses.

"Hold on, are you...?"

"Yes, I'm Sasha," the one on the left answered, revealing a calm, mellifluous American accent as she and her twin sister stood up.

"And hi-hi! I'm Kasha!" the one on the right said, much more excitedly. "Oh, my God, we are such huge fans. When Zahir told us you were maybe going to join the team, we were like, oh my God, we have to meet him. Also, we're on the European leg of our tour, so..."

"Okay, calm down, sis." Sasha threw her twin a censoring look that made me see why Kayla chose Kasha to impersonate when those paps asked her name.

Sasha appeared regal and withdrawn, like an ice sculpture you could look at but not touch. Meanwhile, Kasha had a much more open energy.

Gerald would have called her "accessible." But I supposed the American term would be "girl next door."

I could only think of Kayla, though, as I gawped at the superstar duo. "So, ya don't think this kind of football is borin'?"

"No, *American* football is boring!" Kasha insisted. "European Football is *life!*"

"We enjoyed watching you play," Sasha said with a much more reserved tone.

"And we're so, so excited about you joining our team!" Kasha added, all but jumping up and down beside her twin.

"You're getting ahead of yourself, Kasha." Zahir Zaman finally walked around his desk to join us. "Let us talk to Mr. Atwater about what we can offer him first."

And that's how I found out that Coach Ollie hadn't gone straight to the owner's office to suggest reneging on their proposed offer but proposing that they make an offer right away.

"Obviously, we want your Atomic Foot," Zahir explained after Kasha and Sasha left the office in a flurry of cheek kisses and good-byes. "But we had reservations about your ability to be a team player after the way you were trained up by Greenwich."

"Did Gerald tip you off?" Coach Ollie jumped in to ask. "Because what you showed us straightaway at that practice was we didn't have anything to worry about when it came to you working in sync with the other players. That was, hands down, the best practice we've had since I took over as coach!"

No, Gerald hadn't tipped me off.

But, apparently, me playing nice was exactly what the Paris Triomphe wanted.

And despite bollixing everything from the practice's start time to not playing aggressively enough, I walked out of Zahir Zaman's office with a handshake offer for more than the amount I'd been hoping to get in order to show Greenwich they'd best pay up to keep me on.

I unexpectedly walked out of the meeting having gotten everything I wanted from Paris Triomphe.

And, to my shock, I found Bruno leaned up against the hallway's far wall when I emerged from Zahir's office.

"You're still here?"

"Of course. I am perhaps going to be your new captain, so *oui*, I remained behind as promised to hear your long story."

The old, familiar wall threatened to go back up, but then I thought, *Why not?*

Unlike Kayla, Gerald had actually made the French team sign NDAs that covered every interaction they had with me while I was in Paris.

So Bruno was probably the closest I would get to a confessor who would not run off and tell a gossip site like PureFootball all about it.

And bloody hell, I kinda needed someone to talk to, if only to sort through the mess I was making with Kayla.

So, I told him everything as we headed back to the locker room. Even though I was half afraid Bruno would call me whatever the French version of "twat" was for being this twisted up over a girl I'd only just met.

Instead, Bruno nodded when I finished with my story. "I knew this kind of romance once. An American I met while doing charity work in Eastern Africa. We were both there with an international aid organization, and we grew close, even though our time together was very short. She knew I played football, but she did not comprehend what that meant. I very much liked her not understanding this part of my life."

I nodded, liking the feeling his story was giving me. Suddenly, I understood why the therapist bloke from my anger management course kept going on and on about validation.

"And how'd that end for ya, mate?" I asked, truly interested.

Bruno answered with a Gallic shrug. "Not well. There was a misunderstanding between us, and we never saw each other again." His face darkened with the memory of whatever had happened between him and his American woman.

But then his face relit with an idea as we entered the training room, where the rest of the team was re-suiting up for the last bit of practice after the break. "Actually, I know what we should do!"

He regarded me with an eager look. "Do you mind if I tell the rest of the team your story, too? Sometimes, with big emotional problems, we find it good to talk as a group. How do you put this in English? Perhaps you say, circle up?"

"You want to circle up to talk about my emotional issue?" I squinted at him. "Yeah, you lot are the exact opposite of FC Greenwich. But yeah, mate, why not?"

"*Bon!*" Bruno slapped me on the shoulder, then turned to the rest of the team to give them a much shorter version of my story in French.

To my surprise, instead of giving me the business, suggestions came back in in a mix of French and English—but mostly French.

Eventually, Bruno clapped his hands to signal for them to be quiet. Then he stood up on a bench to deliver another short speech in French.

One that was greeted by a loud cheer.

"What's goin' on, then?" I asked Bruno.

"We were thinking to take you to see one of our most popular burlesque shows after the practice. But I have told them we now have a *new plan*! We are all still going out tonight. But we must find a club with a special VIP section. Very discreet—no paparazzi allowed, just you and us footballers. You will invite your woman. You can tell her it is part of your—how did you call it?—Tourmaline *prize package*? And we will all pretend you are a nobody non-footballer so that you can continue to enjoy her company on your trip."

I shook my head. "And they're cheerin' for that?"

"Mick, *mon ami*, you must understand." Bruno stepped down from the bench and placed a somber hand on my shoulder. "The French do well in three areas, above all others."

He ticked them off on his fingers. "*Les rapports sexuels. L'art dramatique. La duperie.*"

Even with my severely limited French, I understood what Bruno had just said. The French excelled at sex, drama, and deceit.

Still, I squinted at him.

"You understand, *non?*"

"I understand. But you don't think I should just tell her when I get back to the hotel? Come clean about who I really am?"

"*Non! Non! Non!*" came a collective cry.

Bruno and the rest of the team waved their hands in front of their noses as if I'd just farted.

"It is certain she will leave you if you tell her the truth now!" Antoni, the Italian starting goalkeeper, pointed out.

"Show her the very best of times for the next two days and make it so she likes you very much," Hiroki, the Japanese-French defender, insisted.

"*Oui! Oui!*" Bruno agreed with a nod. "You will put on display the kind of life you can provide over these next three days. You must make it so she does not care so much that you are a pro athlete who told maybe a teeny-tiny lie to woo her. This is a good plan, *non*?"

At first, I frowned at them.

Then, I grinned.

"Actually, it's not a terrible plan," I conceded. "And I think I might know just the place...."

CHAPTER 13

Mick

MICK! My guy! No worries, bruh. I got you!

MAX TEXTED BACK IN THAT PARTICULARLY AMERICAN way of his when I asked him for help with the French football club's plan.

That night, Paris Triomphe and their English "prize winner" walked into Kentucky's VIP lounge as Max's exclusive guests of honor.

Kentucky was one of the latest clubs in Max's self-dubbed "50 Clubbin' States" collection—a vanity project of his to open 50 profitable nightclubs named after states in locations all over the world.

"I'm older now. I've got to think of the future," he'd said with mock gravity when he opened his third club, Nevada—ironically not in Las Vegas, where his hotelier family was based, but in London—shortly after his 30th birthday. "I've gotten to the point where I must also get paid to party."

Kentucky was a swank red-and-gold affair located on the same *rue* as the Moulin Rouge. No pictures of any sort were allowed in the entire establishment—not even ussies. The VIP section was ultra-private, totally separated, and hidden away in the back of the club, with its own bar and dance floor. The lounge even had its own bouncer standing guard outside its massive double doors, making the call about who got past the exclusive interior velvet rope.

Magically, even the most beautiful women were turned away at VIP that night unless they were a WAG—married to or dating a member of the Paris Triomphe team.

Also, the WAGs who did get through were quickly "greeted" by Bruno. By "greeted," I mean "given the drill," so that when they came over to Kayla and me—who were sitting together on one of the red velvet settees—they introduced themselves and acted like they had no idea who I was.

I couldn't say for certain about how good the French were at sex. But Bruno had been right about the drama and deceit parts. The Triomphe players acted their parts to a T, making a big show of asking Kayla and me over and over again how we were enjoying France as if they'd never even heard of me before I showed up late to their closed practice. And they also remembered to refer to me exclusively as Mick, not Andy or Atwater.

"Not feeling nearly as special as I used to, now that everybody's calling you Mick!" Max groused under his breath while Kayla chatted with Antoni and his wife, a French fitness influencer/model.

"Don't get jealous, mate," I answered with a grin. "You're still the only American male who gets to call me that."

"Whatever. Your inner circle's starting to look a little crowded," Max grumbled. "What are you trying to do here anyway? Trying to settle down? Like my brother?"

Max wasn't nearly as happy-go-lucky tonight as the last time we'd met up. Apparently, his older brother had decided to get married recently, and, for some reason, that had put him in a truly foul mood.

It probably also hadn't escaped him that there were more wives than girlfriends in the lounge tonight, especially amongst the players who were also in their late twenties like me or their early thirties like him.

He threw a resentful look toward the Triomphe players, who mostly appeared to be chatting and dancing with their partners, paying little attention to the sexy dancers on top of the tables or the scantily clad waitresses discreetly offering products harder than liquor and wine. "So, what? Are these guys, like, your new scene?"

"It's only for the next few days," I reminded him. "After this, I go back to FC Greenwich and revert to the like-nobody bastard you've always known."

That reminder appeared to mollify Max. He switched the subject to some club he planned to open in New Orleans.

But my gut twisted with guilt as I only half listened.

No, I wasn't going to give up my country and the matching deal I'd be getting from FC Greenwich in order to move to Paris.

But I had to admit, it did not feel terrible to spend time with a club that considered themselves a band of brothers, supporting one another rather than rival gladiators, fiercely guarding their spots on the team.

"So, Bruno was telling us you won a prize package, too," Antoni, the Italian goalkeeper, was saying to Kayla when Max and I turned to join into their conversation.

"Mine isn't nearly as nice as Mick's," she shouted over the loud electronic music blasting from all the speakers. "I mean, they flew me out from California, but no extras. Just the hotel and flight. That's it. I'm on my own for experiences, and my room at the Benton Budget is basically a small box compared to his."

"Benton Budgets give their clientele a lot, considering the low price they charge," Max pointed out, projecting his voice much easier than Kayla had. "It's the best American brand in Paris if you ask me."

"Did anyone ask ya, mate?" I replied between gritted teeth.

At the same time, Kayla rushed to assure him, "Oh no, you're right. It's really nice. And super clean. I'm just saying it's no suite at the Tourmaline Paris Étoile. I mean, the room they gave Mick is just bonkers! You should see it."

"Well, you should see the penthouse suites at the Benton Paris Grand...." Max started to counter defensively until I gave him a quelling look.

Having introduced himself simply as the club's owner, without letting on that he was also the playboy scion of the American Benton Hotel Family, it would come off as weird for him to mount such a hard defense of his family's brand.

"Or so I've heard," he concluded with a scowl, dropping the subject.

Kayla uncomfortably took a sip of the fine champagne she had barely touched.

"*In any case, sì,* Mick's package is very generous," Antoni agreed, deftly changing the subject. "We will be taking him to breakfast tomorrow morning, and then he will sit in on another one of our morning practices. But after, I believe there is—how do you say?— a shopping spree at Je T'aime Tourdin, a very nice private-viewing-only boutique in the Golden Triangle. My wife and all of her friends love it. And, of course, Mick should give you this part of his prize so that you can have something nice to wear the next time he takes you out."

"That's a great idea!" I said, quickly picking up on where Antoni was going with this.

I'd borrowed one of the strangely well-tailored formal game-day suits** before coming out to Kentucky with the Triomphe players. But Kayla had to scramble after I texted her to meet me here. She'd spent the first fifteen minutes after her arrival apologizing profusely for her fabric flats and what she'd referred to as her "Kohl's wrap dress."

"This was the only even kind of close to dress-up outfit I could find in my suitcase." She'd eyed the other women in VIP guiltily. As if she'd committed a crime by showing up in a yellow dress when all the WAGs were wearing chic little black numbers.

Truth was, I'd just been happy to see her outside a hoodie.

"You look great, love," I'd assured her. "That bright color's mint against your skin, innit? And the neckline's chef's kiss."

But apparently, Kayla had remained self-conscious about her outfit, if Antoni knew enough to suggest I take her on a shopping spree. Plus, it'd be another opportunity to show her the life I can give her if she just let me.

However, Kayla immediately started shaking her head at the mention of Antoni's made-up shopping spree. "Oh no, I couldn't possibly—"

"Course ya could." I slung an arm around her shoulder. "I'm not one for the fancy togs meself. But ya don't want me to just leave all those shoppin' spree euros unclaimed, do ya?"

I could see Kayla's payroll administrator brain practically buffering under my argument.

"I guess not," she admitted in the end. "And I was planning to maybe look for a few new outfits for work while I was here anyway...."

"*Sì, sì,*" Antoni said approvingly. "Dress for success, as they say."

"I mean, I guess." Kayla glanced at me uncertainly. "As long as it's part of the package and not costing you any money."

"Not a pound," I happily lied, not caring a bit how much dosh this shop Antoni had suggested would cost me.

Strange, I'd spent my entire career avoiding gold diggers who only wanted to spend my money. But here I was, scheming to get Kayla to agree to let me lavish her with gifts.

"Maybe we could go to the Eiffel Tower after the shopping spree tomorrow," she suggested, her tone brightening. "I was planning to go there after the Louvre today, but the line to see the *Mona Lisa* was crazy long! Then I received your text. So, I got dressed as best I could and came straight here without going there. Or, you know, eating dinner."

My arm stiffened around her shoulders, and I exchanged glances with Max and Antoni.

There was no way in hell I could take her somewhere as public as the Eiffel Tower without getting recognized.

"Oh, actually, that tourist trap scene isn't for me," Max said, coming through with an excuse. "How about you, Mick?"

"Yeah, no thanks," I agreed. "Loads of people gathered 'round one structure ain't for me. Plus, I've already been once for a secondary school trip, y'know."

"I, too, visited the Iron Lady during my school days back in Milan." Antoni backed up my story with a knowing nod. "The Eiffel Tower is perhaps a too popular school trip here in Europe. Most of us have already been once."

"And once is all you need for the Eiffel Tower," Max pronounced, his tone dead bored on the other side of me.

"Oh, sure..." Kayla's face fell a little. "You don't want to go again, I understand. That's cool. Yeah, I'm...I'm just going to go use the ladies room now if that's okay."

"Yeah, sure." I stood up with her, appreciating the view from behind as I watched her head toward the "Toilette" sign near the lounge's entrance.

Almost as soon as Kayla was out of earshot, Bruno and the rest of the French team gathered around me, congratulating themselves on their acting.

"Why do we not have our own reality show?" Bruno demanded loudly—in English, but with an extra dose of French outrage in his voice. "We are so very good at this!"

I laughed along with the other players, relieved they'd been able to pull it off as promised.

Not going to lie, I was starting to get caught up in all their camaraderie.

There had actually been movies and docs made about FC Greenwich's particularly violent hooligan Greenie fan base. And that was cos the team tended to produce nutters like meself—real aggro players who could barely stand to be in the same room and talked all the shite if their fellow teammates failed to play their very best.

The Paris Triomphe footballers were a great time, though. Friendly, warm, and able to have fun without chopping up each other's egos or getting into unnecessary pissing contests.

It was easy to sit back down with them and make like we were having a friendly conversation in anticipation of Kayla's return from the loo.

Which was why it took me so long to realize Kayla had yet to return from the toilet.

"Excuse me, mates," I said to the other footballers about twenty minutes after she left. "I'm gonna go check on her."

I saw the problem as soon as I turned the corner where the lounge's single WC lived.

I could easily imagine Kayla making the practical decision to go downstairs to the regular toilets for the rest of the club.

However, there was also a line outside that loo.

Suddenly, I was even more grateful for Kayla's outfit choice.

"Oi, any of you lot seen a Black woman wearin' a yellow dress?" I asked the line of women queued up beside the door of the ladies toilets.

One of the women pointed to a cracked open door at the end of the hallway. Then she asked me something in French.

I didn't understand what she said, but since her question ended in "Andy Atwater," it was easy enough to figure out. Also, after she asked, the other women in line turned and stared.

"Don't speak French," I muttered. Then I made my way to the door at the end of the hallway before anyone could follow up in English.

The door let me out into an alley at the back of the club. *That's strange.* Kayla didn't come off to me as the sort of woman who smoked. But why else would she...?

My heart stopped when I spotted her a little farther down the alley from where the actual smokers were speaking in French and expelling small puffs of smoke into the chilly night air.

No, Kayla wasn't smoking. But she was furiously texting with someone. And from the intent look on her face in the glow of her phone's light, it was obvious that whoever she was texting had her attention. Her full attention.

You're the one who deserves my attention right now. Not him....

With a heart-sickening thud, I remembered what she'd said this morning about transferring her attention from the wanker who was trying to get in touch with her to me.

But that had been this morning.

Kayla had agreed to meet me in the warmth of Max's club. But here she was, outside in the cold. Texting with the ex she said she'd blocked!

CHAPTER 14

Mick

M Y H E A R T T H R E W A W O B B L Y — T A N T R U M I N G I N S I D E M Y chest—as I watched Kayla text with her ex.

She wore the coat she'd checked before coming up to VIP, I noted. That meant she'd intentionally come outside to answer that wanker.

Had I misjudged her? Was she like me mum? Always willing to stick around no matter what kind of abuse me dad dished out to her?

I strode forward, uncaring of the cold winter night. The angry heat in my chest kept me warm as I called out, "Kayla!"

Her head snapped up. And she wore such an obviously guilty expression on her neon-sign face, I knew what I'd suspected was true.

Jealousy kicked a fireball through my chest, and the next words fell out of my mouth like smoke and ash. "You came here to be with me, but you're out here textin' with somebody else!"

Me parents had barely been able to go out to the local without coming home in a screaming argument about some bloke Dad insisted me mum had been flirting with. I hated how much I sounded like him now.

But I had to confront her. "You said ya blocked him, but you've been out here textin' with him the whole time while I've been all over the club, searchin' for you like some trained dog!"

Kayla's expression morphed from guilty to appalled. "Are you kidding me? I wouldn't do that to you! You don't know me from Eve. But tell me you get that I'd never go back on my word like that."

Her fierce denial took a lot of the wind out my outraged sails. I did get that. At least, I thought I did....

"Then why'd ya look so caught out just now?" I demanded, feeling defensive but also a little foolish.

"Because I did come out here to text with somebody. It just isn't Dwayne."

She guiltily turned the phone toward me to reveal a wall of texts. From a contact labeled "Mommy."

The last of my jealousy faded away as I read their back and forth. But I had to ask, "Who're Zephyr and Aziza, and why are you so worried about them?"

"Well... ah... My mom and I are kind of book-clubbing the latest Clara Quinn." Kayla pulled the phone back and returned it to her purse with an embarrassed wince. "Basically, Zephyr is the two-thousand-year-old king of the Wind Fae, and Aziza's the lowly Elemental Fae that he's spent the last three books battling to marry. It was finally going to happen, but at the end of chapter five, she gets kidnapped. We're led to believe by enemy forces—but my mom thinks Aziza's disapproving father is behind it. So... yeah..."

Kayla finished with an apologetic shrug. "I was out here texting with my mom about what's going to happen next when I was supposed to be hanging out with you in VIP. I'm so sorry."

I shook my head and leaned my shoulder against the club's brick wall. "If you were bored talkin' upstairs with us lot, why didn't you just tell me?"

She glanced to the side. "Well, clubbing isn't exactly my jam, and I can only hang out in the VIP section for so long, yelling at the top of my lungs to be heard, before I need a break."

"You didn't answer my question, Kayla." I furrowed my brow at her. "Why didn't ya tell me you were ready to go?"

She tensed, then visibly swallowed. "Well, you looked like you were having a good time with those soccer guys. And I didn't want to bother you just because I was ready to go home."

"*Just because*," I repeated, frowning down at her. "Why do I get the feelin' you're comparing me to your wanker ex?"

"No, I just... I guess I got a little triggered by the Eiffel Tower stuff...." She shook her head, refusing to go on.

But I shook my head right back at her and insisted, "No, tell me. Tell me what you're thinkin' right now."

"It's stupid. I mean, we only have one more night together after this. Why ruin it with real relationship expectations?"

She was trying hard as she could to let me off the hook. But something told me to keep pushing.

"A'right, then. If we was in one of those *real relationships*, if we were all about the communicatin' aspect of things, what would you be sayin' to me now?"

"I don't know." Kayla shrugged. But then her next words came out in a massive rush. "I guess that relationships are give and take. It can't be one person doing all the taking and the other person doing all the giving. If you want me to come out and do the things you want to do—especially on short notice, without leaving time for dinner—you should be willing to do the things I want to do, too."

By the time she finished, her expression had become adorably fierce. I had a strong urge to kiss it off her face.

But first, we needed to sort out this "hypothetical" real relationship issue.

"That how it was between you and Dwayne the Wanker, then?" I guessed. "He'd have you come meet him at some club, and you'd be bored to death, readin' 'bout your thunderstorm fairies and whatnot on your phone while he arsed about with his American football mates."

"Actually, Wind Fae," she corrected. "But other than that, yeah, you pretty much have it right."

She looked down at the ground, visibly ashamed.

"Hey." I took a hold of her chin and tipped her head back up. "I ain't him, a'right?"

"I know," she answered. "I know that. And it's unfair of me to bring baggage from my old relationship into this... whatever it is. I'm sorry."

She tried to lower her chin back down then, but I kept her looking straight at me.

"Nope, you were right. I was being a right knob earlier when you asked me to do somethin' you wanted to do after the shopping spree."

I moved my hand down to her neck so I could stroke her cheek with my thumb. "Thanks for callin' me out on it. I appreciate you comin' out tonight, especially considerin' you were at a good part in your book and all that."

She laughed, but I informed her, "I'm totally serious. Tomorrow night, I'm gonna make it up to ya."

She peeped up uncertainly at me in a way that made me want to follow through on my offer to headbutt her ex. "Seriously, you don't have to."

"Ain't a question of *have to*," I answered. "I want to. Understand?"

All sorts of complicated emotions danced behind her eyes. But in the end, she gave in with a simple, "Okay. I'd really, really like that."

I grinned. "Look at that, our first proper couple row—and we sorted it nice and easy. No shoutin' or beer bottles chucked."

"I, too, am weirdly proud of us," she agreed with a little laugh. "But hey, we should probably be getting back to VIP."

Probably. I could feel the phone I stuffed in my breast pocket vibrating with texts. Most likely messages from Max, wondering why I'd left him alone with a bunch of footballers who weren't truly interested in partying.

But I stayed right where I was with Kayla. "I'd rather spend time with you. Ya get that, right?"

"Right," she agreed with a nod. "Because we only have a couple of nights of sexy times left."

"Not just because of that." I shook my head and stepped closer to her. "I'd rather spend time with you. No matter what we're doin'. Being with you. That's all tonight was supposed to be about."

"Really?" Her face broke into a relieved smile. "I'd rather spend time with you, too. Plus, I'm, like, so, so hungry, and Kentucky doesn't serve any food. I asked."

"A'right, give me twenty minutes," I told her, taking her by the hand. "I've got an idea about dinner."

With that promise, I led her back into the club—not to spend more time with Max and the Triomphe football club, but to chuck them some goodbyes before leaving out.

Also, it gave Kayla the chance to warm up before we scuttled out the back entrance to meet the limo that had replaced the Triomphe car. At least for this evening.

The same driver/guard attended to us, though, and he was already positioned at the new car's back door.

But I waved him off before opening the door to the limo for Kayla meself. I held it open in anticipation of what would come next.

A thrilled screech sounded from inside the car. Then: "Oh, my gosh, I can't believe you did this. Seriously, Mick, you are the best!"

No, *she* was the best.

And I was determined to prove I was worthy of her.

I grinned from outside the car, loving her reaction to my little gift. Loving how she inspired me to be a better bloke. Loving that she'd rather have a quiet conversation with me than enjoy one of the best VIP lounges in France.

Loving...

The voice that had roared in my head so loudly that morning now whispered inside my most secret heart. *Loving her.*

But I tamped down that whispering voice. I couldn't allow meself to consider such a too-fast feeling. Not yet. Not until I proved to her over the next couple of days that I was nothing like her ex, even though it might look that way on paper.

"A'right, then, Kayla," I said, climbing into the back seat with her. "Tell me all about your day, starting with the Louvre."

CHAPTER 15
Kayla

OKAY, ZEPHYR GAVE AZIZA AN EVER-SUMMER GARDEN filled with fireflies as a wedding gift in Chapter 3 of the latest Clara Quinn book. But I'd be darned if I wasn't swooning way more than she did when I found the limo's sideboard bar filled with flowers, a bottle of champagne, and perhaps, most importantly, a ginormous charcuterie board covered in meats, cheeses, bread, vegetables, and both fresh and dried fruits.

And Mick really did seem interested in what I had to say about my day. As we ate the shockingly filling meal of small bites, he listened intently as I told him about hitting the Louvre, along with a couple of cafes.

To my further delight, the limo took us for a bit of a ramble next to the Seine, stopping along the way at a few "tourist trap" monuments that were on my list of places I might want to check out while I was here in Paris.

Mick patiently watched me take picture after picture of the elegant arches and intricate stonework of the Pont Neuf, which, despite its

"New Bridge" name, was actually the oldest standing bridge in Paris, having been built in the 1600s.

"That probably feels like no big deal to you since you also have a really old quote-unquote new London Bridge to look at," I said when we climbed back into the limo. "But there's almost no major infrastructure in L.A. built before the 1900s."

"Actually, the current London Bridge is pretty young. Less than a hundred years old. The old quote-unquote new bridge that replaced the one from the nursery rhyme song's been moved to America now,"," he said, settling back into the limo seat next to me.

"You're joking!"

"How many times do I have to tell ya I don't joke? Look it up on your phone if ya don't believe me. It's in some retirement community or somethin' like that in Arizona. Is this not common knowledge where you come from? I mean, that state's right next door, innit?"

To my shock, Mick totally wasn't kidding.

"In my defense, America is a crazy-big place with lots of crazy-big history," I told him after confirming that the early 1800s London Bridge that replaced the one I used to sing about in preschool was, indeed, relocated in 1968 to Arizona—less than a five-hour drive from Inglewood. "I'll have to go see it when I get back home."

We both grew quiet at the mention of me going back home, and I wondered if Mick was feeling as sad about the notion of never seeing each other again as I already was.

But I'd pasted back on a sunny smile by the time we stepped out of the limo to briefly view the Pantheon from afar. I didn't follow or know much about architecture, but even I could sense the rich history of the former church lit up underneath the Paris night sky.

"Wow! Victor Hugo and Alexandre Dumas are interned there!" I noted after a quick scroll of its history on my phone. "I'll have to make sure to stop back here before the end of my trip. I've never read anything by Victor Hugo, but *The Count of Monte Cristo* was the only book in my AP Lit class that wasn't totally boring."."

Last, but not least, we took a selfie—or an "ussie," as Mick referred to them—

across the river from the equally lit up Musée d'Orsay.

At the last moment, though, Mick turned and blew a raspberry into my cheek, causing me to burst into surprised laughter right as he pushed the red button.

"No, wait, take another one!" I demanded when he immediately repocketed the phone and headed back toward the limo.

"Nah, love, that one's mint. I'll text it to ya!" Mick answered.

Then he ducked back into the limo before I could insist.

Still, after he finally gave the limo driver instructions to head back to the hotel, I had to give credit where credit was due as I slipped off my coat in the overly warm car.

"That was the best, most romantic date ever!"

"Glad ya liked it, but..." He leaned over, and the next thing I knew, his mouth was on my lobe, tugging at it before he whispered in my ear, "Date ain't over yet."

His hand moved down underneath my dress, then slipped between my legs to caress my sensitive inner thigh.

My breath caught at his erotic touch. But... "We can't. Not with the driver right there."

His hand inched even closer to my womanhood, so close I could feel the outside of his index finger against the seat of my panties.

"Yes, right there, behind a tinted partition. If we're quiet, he never has to know." Mick's voice became a challenge in my ear. "Let me see if I can make you come before we get back to the hotel."

My heartbeat quickened at the thought of getting caught doing something as hedonistic as having sex with someone in the back of a limo.

I was a good girl—not the kind of person who had sex in the back of cars. I should have pushed Mick's hand away and told him to stop.

But I didn't.

Instead, I melted into him as I turned toward his seeking lips. I loved the feel of his arm wrapped tight around the back of my neck —keeping me there, wanting me there—as his tongue delved in and out of my mouth.

He moved the crotch of my panties aside, and his fingers began to do the same delving.

"If we're gonna get this done before the hotel, I'm gonna need you to get nice and wet," he murmured against my lips. "Can you do that for me, Kayla?"

The stakes he presented excited me almost as much as the hooked fingers he was slowly pushing and pulling in and out of me. I could feel myself becoming wetter in answer to his question. I could also feel his erection, now hard and unforgiving, against the side of my thigh.

"That's right, love," he whispered in my ear. "Get hot for me. Make this next part one-two-three-four."

I was too turned on to ask what he meant by one-two-three-four. But I soon found out when he removed his fingers from me and unzipped his pants to take himself out. His hard length was already dripping with pre-cum. "One," he said, slipping a condom on over his straining erection.

He easily lifted me onto his lap, with my back to his chest. "Two."

And he just as easily set me down on his long length, invading my slick folds all the way to his hilt. "Three."

He slapped a hand over my mouth as I cried out with the pleasure of being entered so thoroughly. Then, with his other hand, he began rubbing at the nub between my folds on, "Four."

"*Mmmh...*" I tried to stay quiet, but being filled up and touched this way...

I helplessly whimpered into his hand.

"Shh, love," he said in my ear. "I know it feels good, but if you're too loud, we'll get caught."

I didn't want to get caught. I squeezed my eyes closed and bit back on my whimpers, concentrating instead on my breathing and how it felt to have his thick length stretching me to the limit as he worked me below.

Soon, I couldn't take it anymore. I cried out against his hand with the rising sensation. But instead of offering me mercy, he sprawled me back against him, opening me up even further to his touch as I fell apart under his fingers.

The position made me feel like a helpless ragdoll. Barely doing any work but receiving so much pleasure.

However, my pleasure alone seemed to be enough to rev Mick up even further.

"Think I didn't notice when ya rocked up to VIP, wearing a front-clasp bra underneath that amazin' dress? If you knew how bad I've been achin' for ya all day, ya never woulda dared. As it was, you're fortunate I didn't do this in the VIP with everyone watchin'."

I felt a pinch of wicked pleasure at the thought of unknowingly turning him on back in the VIP lounge. But I had to wonder what his threatening "this" referred to.

As if answering my unspoken question, he soon revealed that "this" was him deftly opening the front clasp of my purple bra and pulling open the neck of my yellow dress at the same time, causing my heavy breasts to spill into his large hands.

"Sorry, love, but I can't get enough of these." He palmed my globes in his rough, calloused hands, circling his thumbs around their taut nipples. "How long do ya think I'll be able to last when I finally let meself start movin' inside ya?"

I'd just come, but I moaned at his question. Desire re-pooled in my lower stomach, and some base instinct made me start grinding my hips on his erection.

"I love ya like this, Kayla." Mick's voice became a coarse whisper as he clasped my breasts tightly above my gyrating waist. "Totally exposed. Your knockers hangin' out your dress, so wet I can feel ya drippin' all over me knob, just ruinin' another set of panties."

His lower-class accent seemed to get thicker the more excited he got. "Whaddya think 'ould 'appen if the driver stopped the car and opened the door now? 'Ould you let me keep goin' til you got what you was after?"

The question sent a painful lightning bolt of fresh lust through my body, and I very nearly cried out.

"Shh, love! Remember to keep it quiet back 'ere. Just nod or shake your 'ead to answer me."

I nodded my head, not caring how it made me seem. It was true. At that moment, nothing would have made me stop the journey I was on to another orgasm. The whole city of Paris could be watching us, and I wouldn't be able to stop.

"Look down," he said. "Look down at yourself."

I did. Heaving breasts... purple panties pushed to the side of our joined sexes. My essence glistened on top of my womanhood, which was stretched and straining around his erection.

And as if the image of us like this wasn't erotic enough, he brought one of his hands back down to my sex to complete the picture.

This time, I did cry out. Probably loud enough for the driver to hear. It had been one thing for him to touch me like this when my eyes were squeezed closed.

But the sight of his hand—pale and heavily veined with muscle—moving on top of my dark womanhood? What could I do but cry out and then scream when my release came just a few seconds later? Sharp, alive, and completely mind-splitting!

A deep, triumphant chuckle sounded in my ear. But then he grunted, "Fuck, love, I can't take it no more."

Another warning, as it turned out.

He pushed me forward, just enough to get leverage, and then lost all control. Yanking my head back by my twists, he desperately pumped into my sex.

He'd been such a cruel devil in my ear. But his frantic, sloppy thrusts told me how hard he'd been fighting to hold back while giving me two orgasms.

Make that three.

Something about the way he was taking full and utter possession of me. Fisting my twists as he drilled into me from below. Like I was undeniably *his*. I was so sensitive and primed that another climax crested over me without much prompting.

And soon, my soft cries were joined by Mick's loud shout as he surged inside of me. Then everything fell silent.

There was nothing in the air but the sound of our heavy breathing.

Wait a minute.... There was no sound other than our breath. Why was there no sound other than our breathing?

I lifted up and immediately scrambled off Mick when I realized the car was totally still, with the engine off, obviously parked somewhere.

 "We're not moving!" I said to Mick, who was still sitting in his seat, his face relaxed and blissed out. "Why aren't we moving?"

CHAPTER 16

Kayla

Mick had the good grace to look chagrined as he put himself away and rebuttoned his suit pants. "Well, you see, Kayla, we got to the hotel garage 'bout five minutes ago. But you were too busy to notice."

"And you kept going?" I nearly shouted. But then, realizing we no longer had the benefit of the car engine to mask our conversation, I lowered my voice to repeat, "And you kept going?"

He raised his hands. "In me defense, love, you nodded when I asked if you'd be willin' to go on. As close as ya were, it woulda been unfair of me to stop. I'm not even sure you woulda let me stop. And that's the *Law & Order* truth, both the UK and the US versions."

"I can't believe this!" I reclosed my bra with the speed of a teenage girl caught making out by the police. "Now the driver knows! And, and..."

I looked out the tinted window and spotted an attendant in a hotel uniform standing near the garage door that led into the hotel lobby, obviously waiting for us to get out of the car. I waved a frantic hand toward him. "And whoever that is!"

Mick just laughed. "Kayla, it's fine. They're French. They know what's what."

I held my hand out to him. "Give me your special room key. I refuse to let a butler escort me up like I've done all those other times."

"But I'm right here with ya. Ya don't need a—" he began to say.

"Now! Now! Now!"

"Okay, okay!" Mick handed me his room key, clearly very amused as I jammed my arms through my coat sleeves.

Then, without any further discussion, I put my hand on the door handle and raised my chin high.

I refused to do the walk of shame past the waiting attendant.

I did the *run* of shame. Swiftly opening the car door and racing through the entrance, which the attendant hastily pulled open for me when he saw me barreling toward him.

I was gone and headed back up to the penthouse before anyone could say as much as a *bonjour to me*.

However, that hugely embarrassing incident didn't stop me from introducing a difficult topic with Mick much later that night.

I should have been exhausted. After the three bouts of morning sex, and the Louvre, and Kentucky—the night club, not the state

—and the car sex, then the apologetic round of "I'm Sorry We Got Caught" sex... After all of that, I should have fallen asleep as soon as Mick rolled off me.

But something he'd said earlier had my brain turning and wouldn't let me close my eyes, even after he pulled me in nice and cozy to his side.

"Hey, Mick?" I asked.

"Hmm," he answered.

"You keep saying that you don't joke."

"Cos I don't."

"So, earlier, when you congratulated us on getting through that Eiffel Tower argument? when you said we got it sorted without any shouting or thrown beer bottles? If you never joke, why would you say that?"

He went still. So still, I could tell I had stepped on some kind of emotional landmine. I stilled, too, wondering if he would even answer what I now realized was an intrusive question.

"Your parents, they're the steady, regular type, right?" he asked instead of answering my question. "Nice house, two jobs, three squares a day, church at least every other Sunday sort, right?"

"You forgot lifetime Suns season ticket holders, but other than that, you're right," I answered, smiling at the thought of the two dependable people who'd raised me. "They've been living in the same house forever—they bought in Inglewood before L.A. housing prices got stupid. They're also both career-long members of the Suns Organization. My dad's been a Video Operations Fellow since the Suns taped everything on VHS. And my mom is a Season Ticket Coordinator—hence the lifetime passes."

I sensed Mick would have been happy to listen to me ramble on about my parents forever, but I had to ask, "What are your parents like?"

He went silent again, but not nearly as long as the first time.

Eventually, he answered. "Me dad's worked for the power company all his life, and me mum's been a hairdresser long as I can remember, but they're not like your parents."

He heaved a sigh. "They're the sort who've got to keep movin' from flat to flat cos they get pissed and trash the place. Landlord finds out, and they're on to the next. We moved three times the last year I lived with 'em. Ain't a clue where they're at now cos we don't keep in touch. If I got married or anythin' like that, I'd have to hire a private detective to find 'em. But then I'd never do that, would I? They're not..."

He sniffed in that way men sometimes do when they're trying to prove they're still tough. Or trying to keep it together. "They're not the kind of parents ya invite to posh events. Cos they'd do things like sneak in alcohol to your youth league football games, get blind drunk, then break off 'em beer bottles like they're on one of 'em telly dramas and threaten to off each other with all your teammates lookin' on."

A rock formed in my stomach as he spoke, and it got heavier and heavier the more he said.

I didn't need to be told his description wasn't hypothetical or even hyperbolic. Mick had lived these stories, had lived with these terrible people—was still living with them, even if they hadn't been in contact in years.

I swallowed back tears on his behalf.

But I kept my voice casual when I spoke. "You're right. My parents aren't like yours. Especially my father. He was—still is—a great dad. Always supportive, always there for me. He played high school American football, and he's a big guy, really macho-looking. Plus, he can be a little gruff, y'know? A lot of people are scared of him when they first meet him. But he's a huge teddy bear. He gave my brothers and me all the hugs we could ask for growing up, and he's never picked us up late. Not once."

I entwined my fingers with Mick's. "My dad also never took us to meet his parents. We didn't even know they were still alive until they died in a car accident. Drunk driving. Dad's dad—my grandpa, I guess—ran their car into a pole. Dad told us about them then."

My heart twinged as I thought back to the terrible look on my father's face when he told us that his parents had actually lived nearby in Compton the entire time my brothers and I had been alive.

"We were pretty much the only people that came to their funeral. And a lot of the other people who did come seemed to be way more interested in asking my dependable dad about money they'd loaned his father than paying their respects."

I shook my head. "I couldn't believe those two awful people raised my kind and loving dad. I told Dad that after the funeral, as we were driving home. I was sitting in the back seat between my two brothers, and I'll never forget what he said to me. He said, 'It's easy for me to be a good dad. With every decision that comes up for you three, all I gotta do is think, *What would my parents do?* Then I do the opposite."

Mick's breath hitched underneath our intertwined hands. I suspected he was fighting back tears, but I'd learned enough about him by now to know he wouldn't appreciate me drawing attention to it.

I could envision him as a little boy, his eyes fierce and wide as he refused to cry, even when his parents humiliated him.

So, I continued with my story.

"I wasn't going to go through with this trip, you know. The plan was to spend my vacation days locked away in my room, feeling sorry for myself. But the night before the trip, my dad knocked on my door, wanting to talk. I thought he'd be disappointed about the break-up. The Suns are obviously his favorite team, and I know he wouldn't have minded having an NFL player as a son-in-law. But he was mad at Dwayne. Even madder than I was."

I laughed a little at the memory. "He told me I was better than Dwayne, that I should go on the trip anyway, even if I had to go alone. Then he barged into my room and packed a bag for me—that's why I've been wearing so much Suns' apparel on this vacation and only had one completely inappropriate summer dress. Dad drove me to the airport himself. That's how I ended up coming to Paris alone. And that's why I'm here with you now."

Mick breathed in deeply after I finished my story.

"That's the kind of dad I want to be," he said, his voice husky with emotion. "Not just better—the complete opposite than mine."

"You want kids?" I knew this was just a fling. But the thought of him starting a family with someone else made my heart clamp. Painfully.

"Sure I do," he answered. "But it would have to be with the right person. Someone who wanted them sincerely. Not just to trap me or what have ya."

"Do a lot of women try to..." I started to ask, only to trail off because the answer to my question was obvious.

I'd only known Mick a few days, and the thought of having a child with him made my womb ache. What would it be like to actually date him properly? I could imagine plenty of women resorting to not-so-ethical measures to keep him.

"And your mum?" he asked into my pensive silence. "Tell me 'bout her."

"Oh, she's a great mom," I answered, returning to the subject of my parents with a smile. "We're actually really close these days, but when I was a teenager, we got into a lot of arguments. Now that I'm older, I think that was maybe because—"

"You were too much alike," Mick guessed before I could finish. "She's soft-spoken, loves to read, doesn't like a lot of drama, thinks your dad's a softie, even though everybody else is like, 'Oi, look at that grump!'"

I laughed. "Yeah, exactly. How did you know?"

Mick didn't answer, just pushed our intertwined hands above my head as he rolled on top of me.

His lips found mine, and soon he was pushing into me, his strokes rolling and unhurried. Like he had no destination in mind for us other than making our joining last as long as physically possible.

It was heaven.

But the next day, I woke up alone.

My heart stopped, and I jerked into a seated position in bed, looking all around. Until I remembered what Antoni had said about Mick having to go to a team practice early in the morning.

Letting out a sigh of relief, I picked up the phone I'd remembered to leave charging by the nightstand on my side of the bed—only to have my heart stop again.

There was a message from Mick with an address for where to meet him later that afternoon.

But there was also another message from an unknown number.

Baby, this is Dwayne. Did u block my real number??? The Suns FIRED ME!!! And now I hear you already hooking up with some new guy???? I'm texting you from my mama's phone in Missouri because I need you more than ever. Call me! Call me right now! You at least owe me that.

CHAPTER 17

Kayla

What the heck??? Dwayne got cut from the team???

And you told him about my fling with the Brit???

I FURIOUSLY TYPED OUT A TEXT MESSAGE TO SUZIE FROM the back seat of a French taxi headed toward the Golden Triangle. François had magically had the ride waiting for me at the garage entrance as soon as I arrived in the lobby—I so seriously needed to write the Tourmaline a 5-star review with special mention of the French butler's attentiveness and almost ESP-level intuition.

But I'd barely finished tossing François several *merci beaucoup* before I whipped out my phone to send Suzie my "what the heck" message.

We'd been texting back and forth the entire time I'd been in Paris, and she was the only person I'd told about my impulsive vacation fling.

She'd even taken it upon herself to try to find a Mick or Michael Atwater on social media.

Her last message to me had been a completely serious request to pretty please sneak a peek at Mick's passport or credit card.

> *There are like hundreds of Michael Atwaters in the UK!*
> *Even a middle initial would be helpful to make sure he*
> *doesn't have a string of dead exes he "met on vacation."*

Suzie's true crime podcast addiction was definitely rearing its ugly head. Yet, no mention of Dwayne getting cut from the team.

Completely baffled, I sent through another text message.

> *Why didn't you tell me about Dwayne? And why did you*
> *tell him about Mick???*

Then I waited for her reply as the taxi navigated the busy Paris streets... until I realized when the three dots didn't immediately appear like they almost always did with Suzie, that it was 5 am in L.A. On a Suns Organization payday.

That meant she wouldn't be waking up for several more hours. Even then, there was the morning rush of dropping her son off at his Chinese Immersion magnet school all the way in L.A. proper before coming back to Inglewood. Paydays were always a mess of inquiries, outraged calls, confusion, and various demands.

And I wasn't there to serve as the self-appointed first line of defense before the employees who decided to just show up in person to make their inquiries about their checks reached her office. Which meant she'd be arriving to "a shitshow"—her words, not mine, when she reluctantly approved vacation time, despite it falling over our biweekly payday.

Anyway, I'd be lucky to hear from her before she took her mandatory break to eat her lunch in front of *Scuzz.com on TV*.

But if Dwayne was back in Missouri at his mother's house, he'd probably answer the phone if I called him—also, my questions about how he found out about Mick.

"Madame, we are here at your location, I believe," the driver said from the front seat just when I was considering breaking the bank to make an international phone call to my ex.

"Oh, sorry, thanks!" I put the phone away and pulled out my wallet. "How much do I...?"

The driver held up a hand. "No need, madame. It is all paid for. Perhaps this is the door to the establishment?"

He pointed his hand sideways to a set of teal doors nestled inside an exterior wall of weathered brick. "I will wait here for you to give me a sign that it is OK to drive away."

As I got out of the car and walked up a little cobblestone path toward the doors, I could see why the driver sounded a bit uncertain if he'd taken me to the right place. I had to squint to see the little sliver of a golden sign with Je T'aime Tourdin etched into it.

Beneath the tiny sign hung a much larger one, declaring in both English and French that the shop was private and by appointment only.

I turned to give the French cab driver a thumbs-up. But just as he drove away, a pretty young woman opened one of the doors before I had the chance to push the buzzer. She was tall and the kind of vibrating thin that made me think of L.A. actresses who only ate almonds. She wore her tastefully blonde hair in a refined chignon and her pencil skirt and pretty silk blouse like a uniform.

"I am Isabelle. Right this way, Madame Edwards!" she said, ushering me with an elegant wave of her long, thin hand into a space with glossy hardwood floors and pink-and-silver damask wallpaper. "Monsieur Atwater is already seated and waiting for you."

"Oh, wow..." I said, gaping as I followed her in. "This place doesn't look like any clothing store I've ever seen before."

Beautifully dressed mannequins stood in a half-opened circle in the front of the shop as if they were having a private conversation, not displaying outfits customers might want to buy. In fact, there was more open space than actual clothes. And the sprinkling of settees throughout the space reminded me more of the VIP lounge at Kentucky than a place to shop. There weren't even any counters or cash registers that I could see.

About halfway toward our intended destination, an older woman took me away from Isabelle—who I guessed was some sort of shop hostess. She wore a chic peplum dress and welcomed me in English so rapid, her accent almost sounded British—though way more refined than the kind of English Mick spoke.

"I am Giselle, and I will be guiding you through your shopping experience," she informed me crisply before directing me to a tufted couch with a high back, which was positioned in front of what appeared to be a raised runway.

This was where I found Mick waiting for me, just as Isabelle promised.

He grinned and stood to greet me with a kiss on each cheek as soon as I walked up.

"How ya doin' there, love?" he asked, reintroducing some reality into this situation with his working-class accent.

"Good," I answered, even though guilt twanged in my chest, thinking of the messages I had woken up to a couple of hours ago.

"Did you have a chance to go back to the Pantheon?" he asked.

"Um, no. I actually didn't wake up until late. And then, I was kind of rushing to get ready and here on time...."

I trailed off. I didn't want to lie to him, but I also didn't want to ruin the mood by telling him that Dwayne had tried texting me from his mother's number.

Luckily, Giselle chose that moment to ask me if there was anything I wanted to view from their current collection.

"Um..." Seeing as how I had only just learned of the store's existence the night before, I had no idea about their current collection.

Mick quickly took over.

"Right, fix her up with some business casual since she works in an office, yeah? We'll also take a couple of dresses, somethin' proper-like for a night out. And while you're at it, give us a look at your casual clothes."

I opened my mouth to protest that I already had plenty of casual clothes, but he stopped me with a raised hand. "Nothing against your dad, love, but I'd appreciate seein' you in somethin' other than American football gear."

Giselle tittered, and before I could protest again, Mick sat us down on the store's tufted couch.

Giselle had two assistants also dressed in impeccable black pencil skirts and chic blouses like Isabelle. They magically appeared beside her once we took our seats and pushed flutes of champagne into our hands.

Shopping sprees, as it turned out, took way longer than their name suggested—at least at Je T'aime Tourdin.

After we sat down, actual models started filing out onto the store's raised L runway, pivoting back and forth when they stopped in front of me to show off each dark and well-crafted outfit from the store's current collection at every angle.

"What'd ya think?" Mick asked, after what felt like hours of this, when we were on our second glasses of champagne.

I goggled at him. Even though he was a blue-collar worker, he seemed completely at home and totally unbothered by this experience.

"I wouldn't know," I whispered so I wouldn't hurt anyone's feelings. "All those models are, like, a size zero."

"Right, then..."

Mick set his glass down on a side table and walked over to the runway, where Giselle was standing with one of her assistants.

They had a conversation I couldn't hear from where I was seated. Then Giselle nodded, clapped her hands together twice, and called out something to her assistants in French that had one of them rushing toward the back of the store to open a door discreetly tucked away in the shop's farthest corner.

"What's going on?" I asked as Mick passed by, following Giselle toward the open door.

"Gotta give her my shoppin' spree coupon and all that," he answered without stopping. "Be right back."

Just then, a little old lady appeared with a length of measuring tape around her neck and a pincushion strapped around her wrist. She had me stand up and started taking my measurements.

"Wait—what's happening?" I asked the assistant who'd stayed behind.

"Your . . . ah, friend said you are having trouble deciding, so he is choosing the clothes for you." She pulled out a notepad. "Also, we will need your address so we may send you the clothes when they are ready."

My eyebrows nearly hit my hairline. "Wait a minute. You're tailoring whatever he picks out to fit my exact measurements?"

"*Oui,* of course," the assistant answered as if we lived in a world where fast fashion didn't exist and all clothes were made-to-order.

I had no idea what to say. On one hand, it was weird to have a man pick out my clothes. On the other, it was Mick's shopping spree, so he should be allowed to spend the money however he chose. I guess...

Mistaking my conflicted look for concern, the assistant hastily added, "And do not worry about the dress. We will have it expedited and couriered to your hotel."

THAT WASN'T THE ONLY PRIZE-PACKAGE DELIGHT MICK had in store for me. After the not-so-short spree came to a close, Mick escorted me to the car Tourmaline had given him and directed the driver to take us to the Palais-Royal.

I'd seen the famous landmark sitting across from the Louvre yesterday, but there was so much to squeeze into my trip after Mick left, I hadn't thought I'd get the chance to visit.

To my surprise, not only would I get to see it, Tourmaline provided us with a private tour guide.

As the winter sun dipped below the Parisian skyline, casting a golden hue over the city, I found myself walking with Mick through the Palais-Royal's iconic entrance courtyard, which was dotted with black-and-white columns of various sizes. A knowledgeable historian from a local university gave us the lecture of a lifetime as he walked us through the historic structure, whose interior technically wasn't open to the public since it housed France's Ministry of Culture.

A bunch of council offices, grand rooms with even grander chandeliers, and roped-off salons filled with antique furniture later, my head was practically swimming in the building's history, which used to serve as an epicenter of French culture.

"I can't believe you were going to skip this to watch *Coronation Street* on your laptop!" I hissed behind the tour guide professor's back as we followed him back to the entrance courtyard.

"In my defense, none of this shite sounded more appealin' than a *Coronation Street* catch up before I met you," Mick answered with a hapless shrug.

Did this guy have any idea how swoony every word out of his mouth sounded, even when he wasn't intending to be the most romantic vacation fling in all of history?

I glanced sideways at the man who'd done more for me in 40 hours than my ex had done for me in four years, and suddenly, I was crystal clear on how to respond to all the stuff with Dwayne.

A few minutes later, I dipped into the toilets the professor pointed me to when I asked for a rest stop after our tour was officially done. As soon as the door closed behind me, I pulled out my phone for the first time since I'd met up with Mick for that unbelievable shopping spree.

Suzie still hadn't responded to my messages, but there were four more from Dwayne. Four more I didn't bother to read.

It didn't matter that Suzie hadn't responded. She didn't have to for me to be certain of my next move with Dwayne.

I reported the text messages as junk and blocked his mama's number, too.

"You look happy," Mick said when I emerged from the women's toilets.

"You know why I'm happy, right?" I asked, taking his arm as we resumed walking out of one of the wings of Palais-Royal that people rarely got to see.

"Cos of me?" His tone lay somewhere between hope and pride.

"Cos of you," I happily confirmed.

I FOUND OUT WHAT THE SALES ASSOCIATE FROM JE T'aime Tourdin meant about having the evening dress Mick chose for me expedited and couriered when the suite's doorbell rang shortly after I finished taking a pre-dinner shower.

I answered to find François holding a pink-and-silver damask dress bag with the exclusive store's logo scrawled across it in gold letters.

I thanked the French Butler and took the delivery back to the bedroom just as Mick emerged from the bathroom with a towel wrapped around his waist. "What ya got there?"

"The dress you picked out for me," I answered, my voice going a little weak.

The sight of him in nothing but a towel distracted me from my intention of hanging the bag up on the closet door's hook so that I could unzip it.

"By the way, are you aware you have a ridiculously nice body?" I asked a little breathlessly. "I mean, none of the guys I see tending the power lines in my neighborhood look like you."

He grinned. "So that's why you're with me, then? You're just usin' me for me body?"

"No, I'm with you because you're easy to be with and because you're really great. I'm just saying, the body doesn't hurt. You're more ripped than some of the players on the Suns."

"More—how'd ya call it—'ripped' than Dwayne the Wanker?" he asked.

I rolled my eyes. "Yes, more ripped than him."

Mick visibly preened but dropped the subject with a, "Well, go ahead and put on the dress, then. I'm starvin', and we've got to be there in less than an hour."

I had no idea where *there* was. Some fancy restaurant he'd assured me was covered by the prize package but definitely wouldn't let me in wearing any Suns' apparel.

I unzipped the bag and almost let out an audible gasp.

"You shouldn't have. You really shouldn't have," I said, pulling out a vibrant, deep-red statement dress.

It featured a ballgown silhouette with a low sweetheart, off-the-shoulder neckline on top. But then a whimsical cascade of what looked like handstitched flowers descended from its cinched waist to form a voluminous floor-length skirt.

I had never seen—much less worn anything so finely made in my life!

"I mean, how much did this cost?" I demanded. "Was it really all covered by the shopping spree?"

"Put it on, love," he said, ignoring my questions. "I want to see it on you."

That's when I noticed the second hanger behind the first. It had a bustier made up of the prettiest pale-yellow lace I'd ever seen and matching short briefs made of the same material. "And you got the underwear, too?" I shook my head. "I really don't think I can accept this. Or at least let me pay the taxes on it. I mean, there's no prize package in the world that would cover the taxes, too!"

Mick closed the space between us, and without a word, he untied the sash of the robe I'd put on after my own shower, exposing the full length of my naked body to his hooded eyes.

"This is why I took over at Tourdin, ya know." He palmed my naked breasts with his large hands before slipping the robe off my shoulders. "You're the sort who never buys anythin' for herself. And I'm the sort that won't let that stand."

With that, he unclipped the lacy underwear from the hanger and held it out at my thigh line. "Step in."

I stepped in, putting a hand on his shoulder to maintain my balance as I did. "Seriously, I don't need you to help me get dressed. I was just saying..."

I cut off when he let his hand skim over the V shape between my legs, an errant finger dipping into my tunnel.

"I know what you were 'just sayin',' " he said, sliding his finger in and out of me on each word.

I let out a little moan, but instead of finishing, he removed his hand from my sex and pulled the delicate pair of briefs up and over my butt.

Then he turned me around toward the room's mirror so he could put on the matching bustier.

As he connected the hooks, I could feel his erection through the towel, heavy against my back. But after he was finished, he merely turned away from me, took the dress off its hanger, and unzipped the back.

"Step in," he said again.

I did as I was told, but I was disappointed when he simply pulled the cocktail dress up my body without any further intimate touches.

Still, the dress fit like a hug. I stood in front of the mirror, mesmerized by my image after I pulled my twist into a high bun, elegant enough to match the beyond gorgeous dress.

"Close your eyes," Mick said after I was done with my hair.

I did, and I heard him walk away and open a nearby drawer. He quickly came back and clasped something around my neck.

"Now open 'em again."

This time my gasp was audible. A waterfall of multicolored jewels now adorned my neck, falling all the way to my cleavage.

It was less a necklace and more of a statement piece. Colored glass meant to dazzle. There was no way the green jewels could be emeralds, the blue jewels sapphire, and so on. But even as a well-designed piece of costume jewelry, the necklace was no less stunning than it would have been if it was the real thing. I could only gape at my image in the mirror.

My speechless reaction seemed to please Mick as he wrapped his arms around me from behind. "Got it from the shop downstairs. Don't ask me how much it cost. This is our last night together. Let me give this to you."

Maybe it was because I had never in my life seen a necklace so beautiful or because he was right—it was our last night together, and I didn't want to spend it arguing about his questionable spending on me.

For whatever reason, I put my payroll administrator brain aside and said a simple "Thank you."

He turned me around in his arms, but before he could kiss me, I stiffened.

"What?" he asked.

"This dress is so nice, but..." I grimaced. "There's no way I'm going to get away with wearing my fabric flats with it."

It seemed that everything was easily acquired in Paris.

François delivered a pair of golden heels in my size to the suite just a few minutes later.

A pair of heels with red bottoms!

"One last night," Mick reminded me with a warning look when he caught me checking the label.

So, I didn't argue, but I did vow to myself that I'd look up how much they cost, then go downstairs early tomorrow morning and discreetly pay for the shoes, the necklace, and anything else Mick had tacked onto his Tourmaline room bill before I picked up breakfast for us.

It was the least I could do, considering how generous he'd been about sharing his prize winnings with me.

Still, after he put on a tuxedo that I could only hope he'd rented, I had to wonder just where he was taking me.

"This restaurant you made reservations at--it's so fancy you have to wear a tuxedo?" I asked him in the elevator as we made our way down to the car.

"Yep, that's what the prize package said."

"What's the restaurant called again? Maybe I ran across it on TV. My mom loves those international cooking shows."

"The Third Level."

"Hmm, never heard of it." I reached for the phone in my purse to look this restaurant up.

But Mick took my hand in his before I could. "Let it be a surprise, okay?"

My heart let out a little sigh at his request. Seriously, was it even possible to deny this amazing man anything?

"Okay, fine," I agreed.

But "let it be a surprise" turned out to be an understatement.

My chin nearly hit the floor when the car let us out in front of the Eiffel Tower.

"I told you I'd make yesterday's dinner up to you," Mick said with a grin.

Yes, he did.

After a ride in two brightly colored hydraulic elevators with exposed wheelworks, I discovered "The Third Level" was actually the third observation platform at the top of the tower.

People came from all over the world to see Paris from the tower's highest observation deck, but tonight it had been closed off to the public.

A table set for two awaited us, with the most stunning view of Paris in the background.

CHAPTER 18

Mick

THE LOOK ON KAYLA'S FACE, WHEN I SAT DOWN ACROSS from her at the private observation deck table, was worth everything I'd had to do over the past twenty-four hours to make this special dinner happen on such short notice. Including the one, I knew my agent, Gerald, would be none-to-happy about.

An FC Greenwich player could not get a private table set up on the Eiffel Tower's most popular observation deck. But as a future member of the AS Paris Triomphe, the city was mine to do with as I pleased.

"Are you serious?" Kayla asked as soon as the maître d' who had seated us disappeared behind the enclosed observation deck's wood-and-glass doors. "You can't be serious."

"I told you, I don't kid," I answered.

"I know, but this is..." She suddenly reached across the table and grabbed my hand. There were tears in her eyes. "Thank you."

"Don't cry, love," I said, reversing the hold and enclosing her hand in both of mine. "You deserve it."

But Kayla shook her head. "Not after I got on you last night about not coming to the Eiffel Tower with me. I mean, you were planning to surprise me with this prize package gift all along? Mick, I feel horrible."

So did I.

I'd been throwing money at her all day in one way or another, yet it was doing nothing to assuage my guilt over continuing to lie to her. In fact, the more money I spent, the worse it became.

But I was going to tell her after this dinner, so...

I distracted meself with picking out a bottle of wine, which we drank slowly as we made our way through several courses. Throughout dinner, I pretended to be just like her, a middle-classer enjoying a luxury sweepstakes experience in Paris... until we finished up the dessert course.

After the waiter delivered our *cafés*, I knew the time had come to tell her.

"Kayla, look...."

"Yeah, I know, can you believe it?" she answered, turning away from me before I could finish.

It took me a few blinks of confusion to realize she was talking about the scene of Paris all lit up below us. She'd mistaken my "look" as a command.

"Just when I think this city can't get any more beautiful, we get to see it like this." Kayla clasped her hands to the necklace I'd bought her and released a happy sigh. "I'm seriously falling in love with this city. Actually..."

She looked away from the view and turned back to face me. But I could still see the lights of Paris sparkling in her eyes when she said, "I think I'm falling in love with you, too."

Jesus Christ. My heart violently constricted in my chest.

The close-to-death feeling must have registered on my face because she gave me an apologetic grimace.

"I know it's too soon. And I know we only just met each other. And I know that it's impractical to feel this way since you're leaving tomorrow, and neither of us have the money in real life to be flying back and forth from London to L.A. all the time."

For a moment, I couldn't talk because so many words were stuck in my throat.

But my silence made more words come spilling out of her mouth. "I'm sorry. Really, I shouldn't have said anything, just kept my feelings to myself. But this is the best time I've ever had in my whole life, and I couldn't let you go home without telling you that."

Finally, I was able to speak. "Don't apologize to me ever again!"

She blinked, obviously taken aback.

"Okay," she said carefully.

"You're always on with the 'I'm sorry,' and you've never done anythin' to be sorry about. Not one thing."

Her eyes melted. "Oh, Mick, that is so sweet..."

"And you should know that..."

My throat worked. But instead of the speech I had planned, words I didn't think I'd ever say to anyone slipped out. "I love you, too."

"Really?" A smile broke out across Kayla's face, and it was nothing short of beautiful.

"Yeah, really," I answered. *Easily.*

"Me callin' you 'love' ain't just a British thing," I added quietly, though I knew confessing this made me look like a romantic idiot.

161

"I've been feelin' the real thing for you—since the moment ya showed up at me hotel room."

Kayla clamped her lips, her entire expression going a little gooey.

But then she said, "I'm sorry, but I'm going to have to break your new 'don't apologize' rule...."

"Seriously, Kayla—" I began.

Only to have her interrupt me again. "I'm sorry I didn't tell you I was falling in love with you sooner."

Fuck.

Me.

She loved me. And I loved her back.

There was no way I was gonna tell her the other thing I had planned.

This night was the perfect end to the perfect day.

I wouldn't—I *couldn't* tell her. Couldn't ruin this moment. Not yet.

Love!

For me, the sex we had that night felt like a living manifestation of our Eiffel Tower confession. Every touch sizzled with it. Every kiss labeled it by name. I loved her breasts, suckling each peak in my mouth for minutes on end.

Then I moved down to the V shape between her legs, my mouth spelling out our love with every flick of my tongue until she came for me hard, pushing into my still-hungry mouth.

"I wanna know where Dwayne the Wanker ever got off makin' you think you ain't perfect?" I demanded when I came back up to kiss her lips. "You know what you taste like, Kayla? Woman. Joy. Love. If my prick wasn't such a selfish bastard, I'd stay down there all night. Don't laugh. You know I ain't jokin'."

Her laughter transformed into a soft gasp when I pushed into her. She moaned, her hands finding my hips as I braced meself and established a rhythm.

"Open your legs wider, love. I want to go deeper."

She did as I said, her hands moving to my bottom.

I groaned when I sank further into her—then I resumed my ride with monstrous, claiming thrusts.

Chanting, "I love you, I love you, I love you..."

"Mick! Oh, Mick!" Kayla went wild underneath me, bucking and squirming, until she managed to babble a few words, telling me how good it felt, how she had never experienced anything like this before.

The same was true for me. But I couldn't have put words to my feelings if I tried.

I wished for crazy stuff, like that I hadn't put on a condom. I wished for us to make a child together, a girl with her good nature and my athletic ability. I wished we could get married before she left so she'd have a reason to quit her job and come right back to my side of the Atlantic to be with me forever. I wished we could defy the laws of physics, that I could sink deeper and deeper into her until we became one.

I released then, with a great yell, all of my wishes spilling out of my body and flooding into the condom. "I love you so much, Kayla!"

Somewhere in the distance, I heard her say, "I love you, too!"

It took us both a long time to come down from that. We clung to each other for what felt like hours, whispering "I love you" back and forth as I clasped her tight against my chest.

"Mick?" she asked.

"Yeah, baby," I answered, hoping she didn't ask me to let up on my hold. I didn't know if I could, especially considering this would be the last chance I'd have to hold her like this.

Because tomorrow, when I left for London, I'd be forced to tell her the truth—who I was and how I'd been lying to her this entire time. This fantasy we had created together would all come crashing down around me.

But then she said, "I know it's hard to get unscheduled time off when you work for the government, but do you think you could stay? Just for a few more days? Until my trip is over?"

I WENT TO SLEEP THAT NIGHT FEELING LIKE SOMEONE who'd been granted a stay of execution—even though agreeing to Kayla's request for me to stay through the end of her trip was going to get me in a heap of trouble with FC Greenwich.

I could only imagine the hell the coaches would be giving me, especially after Gerald called to tell them I would not only be returning to practice late but would also not be giving them an opportunity to negotiate my contract for next season.

But none of that mattered, did it?

Saying yes to Kayla's request had effectively given me three more days. Three more days to woo her, like Bruno and the rest of the team suggested. Three more days to figure out how to tell her who I really was.

And yeah, sure, I'd have to figure out a way to make her agree to continuing our stay at the Tourmaline, where I wouldn't be in constant threat of being mobbed by paps and fans. Also, without the prize package to fall back on, I'd have to figure out a good excuse for why I couldn't go to any major landmarks with her over the next few days.

However, I had faith that Bruno and Zahir Zaman would continue to weave their magic, especially now that I would be an official member of the club starting in August.

None of those obstacles mattered. All that mattered was me getting to spend more time with Kayla before she went home to California.

However, when I woke up the next morning in the bed that would be ours for three more days, one thing was missing. Kayla.

Her side of the bed was empty except for a notepad on her pillow with 8:00 a.m. written in the corner of the top sheet.

Going down to the restaurant to grab us some breakfast. Will probably be back before you

I shook my head, guessing that she'd opted to make the trip herself rather than tack another room service charge on our bill. But why hadn't she finished the note?

That was when I saw the phone lying next to the note. Still connected on its long charger.

As if Kayla had gotten a message on it while she was writing the note to me.

Gotten a message and thrown down the phone, leaving it behind when she dashed out of the suite.

Listen, I wasn't looking to add to my long list of red flags where Kayla was concerned. But some male instinct made me pick up the phone, knowing that I'd find the reason for her hasty exit there.

What I saw caused my heart to flatline.

Several missed call notifications and two text messages waiting on the front of her still-locked screen. One from Suzie and the other from an unmarked number.

> *SUZIE: Girl, you are on vacay with a fine Mr. Right Now! Stop worrying about Dwayne!*
>
> *314-555-9876: You block my mom's number too??? That's bullshit!!! Choosing some player u just met over me! Well, guess what? I'm n Paris! Down here n the Tourmaline lobby. So now ur gone have to talk to me.*

CHAPTER 19

Mick

I SPOTTED THEM AS SOON AS I STEPPED OFF THE PRIVATE penthouse elevator with Kayla's phone in my hand.

My heart plummeted at the sight of the woman I loved. She was dressed in a Suns hoodie and a pair of sweatpants, with the team's name written down one leg, and clung to the handle of her large purse as she spoke animatedly with the French butler whose name she'd insisted I commit to memory, François.

Well, Kayla didn't look nearly as happy with his performance as she did when she made me promise to remind her about leaving a review before we left the hotel last night. And even worse than that, there was a bloke who was not me standing at her side.

I immediately recognized him as her ex, Dwayne. Even if Bruno hadn't insisted on looking up a picture of "the enemy" yesterday at breakfast while we were plotting my perfect last day of activities with Kayla, I would've known who he was due to him being dressed from head to toe in L.A. Suns gear.

He had that classic bench-warmer physique. The football tights he wore underneath athletic shorts showcased his muscular legs. But the tight, long-sleeved yellow thermal top he wore underneath an orange sideline cape coat strained around his belly paunch. Clearly, he hadn't kept up with the necessary core work to assure a strong kick for the few times he was called off the bench.

However, that didn't bring me much solace as I approached the scene.

Dwayne and Kayla looked like a couple as she confronted François.

"Tell me!" she was saying to François. "Tell me the truth right now!"

"Madame, please calm down," François said. "If you will just follow me, we can call Monsieur Atwater, and perhaps he can—"

"Perhaps he can do what? *Lie to me* some more? I mean, what the heck?!"

She vaguely waved her hand in the direction of the lobby's overhead flatscreen television, which was broadcasting a news program.

I quickly recognized it as the same type of football morning sports highlights shows we broadcast in England. Except in this French version, the announcers were talking excitedly while a cartoon graphic of me wearing a Paris Triomphe jersey, along with my usual perma-scowl, stood with arms folded at the bottom-right side of the screen.

On the top-right side of the screen, video of Kayla and me ran on a loop. Me getting in the car outside of Kentucky, entering Je T'aime Tourdin. They even had a video of us giving each other a kiss as we left the Eiffel Tower.

What had happened was immediately obvious. Someone had leaked the news of me agreeing to join the Paris team. And now this French sports program was discussing not only the highlights of my career, but also the mystery woman I'd been running all over Paris with.

And maybe even that wouldn't have been enough to tip off Kayla, but obviously her ex had also found out about us. Probably via some sports gossip site that catered to sports afficionados on both sides of the pond.

"Why would you help him do this to her, man?" Dwayne demanded loudly beside Kayla just as I'd almost reached them. "Did he pay you? Is this, like, some kind of Frenchie thing?"

"Madame, monsieur, please. Do not make a scene," François pleaded. "We can talk about this privately. Please come this way."

François attempted to take Kayla by the arm, but Dwayne got between them. "Don't you think you already did enough? Kayla's suing you, him, this hotel, and anybody else who had anything to do with this."

"Andy!" a French voice called out from a cluster of seats in the lobby. "Andy Atwater! The Atomic Foot! It is really him!"

I stopped short as nearly everybody in the lobby turned to look at me.

Including Kayla and Dwayne.

Somewhere in the distance, cheering broke out, with quite a few French men chanting my name. But I could barely hear them.

Everything went quiet in my head as Kayla walked toward me. Her expression was horrified and disoriented. Like someone who had just witnessed a bombing.

"All these people chanting your name?" She shook her head at me. "And according to Dwayne, there's pictures and video—actual video of me all over the sports gossip sites?"

"Kayla, let me explain. There's been a misunderstandin' between us from the beginnin'."

"No, you don't need to let him explain nothin', Kay!" Dwayne insisted beside her. "Let your lawyers explain when you sue him for everything he's got!"

Kayla threw him an annoyed glance. "Stop, Dwayne. You are not a part of this. This is between me and *Andy*, and I just need to understand...."

She turned back to me, her eyes completely devoid of the love that had shined so clearly in them the night before at the Eiffel Tower. "So when you told me you were an electrician, that was a *misunderstanding*?"

"I said I came from a family of electricians. Never said I took that path meself."

"And when I told you *explicitly* that I would never want to date a pro athlete?" Kayla's expression fluctuated, as if a s was threatening to erupt underneath her face. "Was that a misunderstanding, too?"

Brain scrambling, I dredged pieces of the speech I'd planned to make last night.

"I hoped that if you got to know me..."

"You *hoped* that if I got to know you, I wouldn't mind you lying to me from the very beginning?" Kayla exploded. "Because that's what you did! There was never any Tourmaline prize package. You went out of your way to convince me you are someone you're not. And apparently, you even got the entire French soccer team to help you do it. All so you could... what?!"

She threw her arms out to the side. "Get in my pants?"

"I mean, the Tourmaline Group did front the bill for the hotel suite and the flight," I said cos that was the only point I could really refute.

Christ, this was getting out of hand.

Kayla was looking at me like I was a murderer of small children. And I could see several phones pointed in our direction out the side of my eye—a few of which, no doubt, were set to record.

"You lied to me!" Kayla's sweet voice went guttural and ugly. "From the beginning! Will you at least admit to that?"

The utter disappointment in her eyes was so disheartening, it actually made me want to lie to her again.

A thousand new fibs sprang to my mind—anything to keep her, to preserve what we had. I thought of how happy we had both been just a few hours ago, and desperation nearly overtook me.

But in the end, I knew I couldn't.

Cos there was one thing I'd said that had been the complete and utter truth.

I loved her. I truly did.

Too much to continue with this charade, even though I knew what a full confession would cost me.

"Yeah, Kayla, I lied to you," I admitted in front of her ex and everybody else watching with their phones out. "I lied to you. I've been lyin' to you this whole time. Cos, Kayla, I knew…"

I swallowed the bitter truth down. "I knew that if I told you everythin', you wouldn't understand that I was the exception to your new rule. You'd push me away cos you're afraid. Even last night, when you claimed to love me, I knew you didn't really mean it. Not truly."

Kayla's face contorted with fury. "I only claimed to love you because I didn't have any idea who you were!"

"You know exactly who I am!" I exploded back. "You are the only woman I have ever shown the real me."

"The *real you*?" Kayla practically spat the question. "Everything you told me was a lie! I fell in love, way too soon, with a lie!"

"Say what you want, but you know that's just an excuse," I insisted, shaking my head.

"That's the real reason you stayed with this wanker for as long as you did, innit?" I said, indicating Dwayne.

"Hey!" Dwayne yelled.

But I pushed on with my point as if I didn't hear him. "Because he was safe. Cos you thought he was some nice Missouri boy, and you were afraid of dating someone you felt something real for. Someone like me!

"You're a coward when it comes to us. You have been from the start. You only fell in love with me cos you thought I was safe. That's why I couldn't tell ya. Cos I knew, when I did, this would be how it ended between us. And I was right."

I pointed angrily at the floor. "You're usin' me being a pro athlete to do what you've been wantin' to do from the start. Run! Run like the coward you are. Especially when it comes to us."

She stared at me.

Then stared at me some more.

Then she slapped me so hard that my face turned sideways.

A great gasp went up all around us.

But, Kayla, who was usually so self-conscious, just ignored them and snatched her phone out of my hand.

"I'm not going to sue you, *Andy*," she informed me, her voice low and harsh. "Because I never want to see or deal with you again."

With that, she stormed past me toward the lobby doors.

"Wait—you can't leave," I called after her. "What 'bout your suitcase? It's still in me room."

"Keep it," she said, swiping at her angry tears as she made her way to the lobby doors. "That's what I should have said three days ago!"

She ran out of the hotel, then, and Dwayne followed.

"Kay! Kay! Wait up!" he called after her. "Where we goin'?"

It hadn't gone as bad as I'd been imagining when I tried and failed to tell her the truth.

It'd gone even worse.

For several moments, all I could do was stand there. Then the voice screamed inside of me.

Go after her! Make her understand!

I tried to do that. I did.

But as soon as I stepped a foot outside the hotel, I was swarmed by paps and new Parisian fans seeking autographs.

They'd let Kayla by, but they surrounded me with demands and questions, making it impossible for me to get through them. It left me with no choice but to stand there, helpless and trapped, while Kayla hailed a cab and jumped in with Dwayne.

Speeding out of my life.

Forever.

Kayla

DESPITE MY DRAMATIC EXIT, I DIDN'T END UP LEAVING everything behind in Paris.

Dwayne, however, was ditched soon after our taxi's arrival at the Benton Budget.

"Are you serious?" He grabbed my arm after I thanked him for the information and tried to leave him behind on the curb in front of the hotel's entrance.

"I came all the way to Paris to get you back. Do you know how much that cost me? I don't even have enough money to pay my rent next month in L.A.—especially without a job!"

Old Kayla would have felt guilty about Dwayne's plight.

But new Kayla's head was still spinning with anger and outrage over what had happened with Mick—Andy—whatever his name was!

I snatched back my arm and shut down Dwayne's guilt trip with a scathing, "I am not responsible for your poor decisions—not when we were dating and most definitely not now that we're done. I am never taking you back, so get that dream—really that nightmare out of your head."

At first, Dwayne blinked at me, looking like a confused 5 foot 11 child.

Then he started to cuss me out.

"Not your fault? Not your fault? It's all your fucking fault, bitch!"

With a numb heart, I turned away and headed toward the hotel's double set of front sliding doors.

"I'd still be on the Suns' roster if it wasn't for you not under-standing the difference between me cheating on you for real and a publicity stunt! I had to do it—*for my brand*! Why the hell can't you—what? No, stop! Get your hands off me!"

Dwayne abruptly switched from yelling after me to yelling at a broad-chested security guard when the middle-aged man blocked him from following me through the second set of doors.

"Guest only. Right this way, Monsieur!" The guard escorted Dwayne out of the hotel so smoothly that I could tell I wasn't the first tourist in Paris who'd needed his help to ditch her trifling ex at the curb.

After that, I settled back into the room I should have been staying at all along, and I had no problem blocking the third number Dwayne had tried to reach me at in as many days.

However, my thumb hesitated over the option to delete and block the contact I'd made for Mick.

But then I reminded myself his name wasn't Mick, it was *Andy*.

Specifically, Andrew Michael Atwater—or, as PureFootball.com referred to him when they placed him right below some guy named Roy Keane on their list of *7 Meanest British Footballers of All Time,* "The A.M. Volcano."

Just a little bit of research yielded a slew of articles detailing his horrible me-first attitude, his refusal to commit to any of the many celebrity women he'd been linked to throughout his soccer career, and his billion-dollar "side hobby" of making ruthless business deals when he wasn't on the field.

The more I read, the more I understood why he'd pursued me so hard. I'd been a pawn in his latest business deal, the perfect cover story—and plaything while he negotiated what appeared to be a significant payday to defect to the Paris Triomphe team next season. That night at the VIP Lounge might have been some kind of hazing ritual, for all I knew. "The A.M. Volcano" testing his new teammates to see just how far they'd go to acquire him.

Andy—not Mick—had been using me. I erased and blocked the contact without another moment of hesitation.

Then, I put all of my energy into doing what I should've from the start, planning out an itinerary for my last three days in Paris—which I'd get back to after a quick run to the closest discount store to pick up enough clothes and toiletries to get me through the rest of my trip.

However, that turned out not to be necessary. The hotel manager knocked on my door a few minutes later with my two suitcases. Apparently, François had packed for me and sent everything I'd left in their penthouse suite over to my room at the Benton Budget.

Just like that, the cute little back and forth with my luggage was solved by an efficient butler—obviously following the orders from a ruthless player who didn't need me anymore to pull off his plan.

My eyes grew hot—but no, I refused to cry.

Crying was what got me into this position in the first place.

I could just imagine Mick looking at me on that plane, vulnerable and so stupidly honest. I'd cried myself straight into his evil mind games.

"Thank you," I said to the hotel manager, lifting my chin. "Let me just go grab my purse for a tip."

"Ah, no, madame," she answered. "This will not be necessary. Actually, there is something I must talk with you about..."

AND THAT'S HOW I ENDED UP ACCEPTING AN ECONOMY trip ticket home to L.A. on a flight leaving the next morning.

The only slightly apologetic manager had firmly explained that paparazzi and other reporters had begun to arrive at the Benton Budget.

"We do not have the personnel to handle such events here, and our normal security is not enough."

She'd also advised that trying to do "the usual tourist things" would be much more difficult, given the furor over the acquisition of "The Atomic Foot"—also because of that huge scene we made at the Tourmaline.

"Excuse me, but this event is already being talked about on many news sites?" the manager explained. "I have been authorized to procure a ticket home for you—or perhaps you would like for us to move you into a suite at our Benton Grand location?"

"No, no more suites!" I answered. "I'll take the ticket!"

So, in the end, I came home with my suitcases. But my dignity, both intimate relationships I've had in the past four years, and my general sense of trust???

Well, all that got left behind in Paris.

However, the story followed me home.

It was true that Americans weren't big on soccer. It might be a huge sport everywhere else in the world, but it was barely even covered in the States unless a major match, like the World Cup, was involved.

Prior to my return to California, I could have argued that, like me, few Americans would be able to pick Andy "Mick" Atwater out on the street—or in first class.

A soccer player could literally get in several game fights like Andy apparently had, and it still wouldn't make the stateside news cycle. Nothing but the most niche American sports gossip sites, that only people like Dwayne read had picked up the story about Mick enjoying a romantic holiday with an unknown American in Paris.

But the story about an American being strung along by a famous British soccer player after being publicly cheated on by her American football player ex?

Well, that caught traction.

All over the world.

Eff. My. Life.

Just a few days after my return, clips and posts about me slapping "The A.M. Volcano" in the Tourmaline lobby from just about every angle had caught fire online.

I found out the hard way that a news story like that would definitely get picked up by *everybody*.

By the time I returned to work the following Monday after my supposed "vacation," I could barely walk through the office under the weight of my coworkers' pitying stares.

Had I thought I knew what humiliation was when Suzie showed me footage of my boyfriend making out with a reality star on an afternoon gossip show? Ha!

That had just been a little prick. The fallout from the Paris fling had come with humiliation that felt like getting stabbed in the chest.

The Monday night after my disastrous return to work, when I headed toward the garage to put in a long overdue load of laundry, I even caught my parents and my college-aged brother watching Gary Berry, their favorite late-night host, send up the argument during the 8:35 p.m. east coast feed broadcast of the L.A. Based show.

"As a huge Suns fan, nobody was more shocked than me that the Wisconsin Bears made it into the division slot for the Big Game," Gary Berry told a live audience during his top-of-show monologue. "Frankly, I thought they were in the Playoffs Choke Club like us! It kind of felt like they were just pretending to be a team that had absolutely no chance of going all the way. I actually have footage of me confronting tonight's guest, Wade Winters, in the green room about it. Watch!"

In the clip, Gary, dressed in the exact same head-to-toe Suns gear and crossbody canvas anti-theft purse I'd been wearing that fateful morning in Paris, walked into the green room with the show's band leader, who sported football tights, athletic shorts, a Suns thermal, and a huge sideline cape like Dwayne.

Together, they confronted Wade Winters, the handsome quarter-back of the Wisconsin Bears.

"Let me explain, Gary," Wade pleaded."

"Why? So you can lie to me some more?" Gary spread his arms just like I did during that confrontation. "I should've known never to trust a pro athlete!"

The argument went on from there with an almost line-for-line parody of the one I had with Andy Atwater in the Tourmaline lobby.

My parents watched in grim silence, but Stevie laughed throughout the bit. And he just about fell out when Wade yelled, "Yeah, Gary, I lied. I've been lying this whole time. Cuz, Gary, I knew... I knew that if I told you everything, you wouldn't understand that I was the exception to the choking during the playoffs rule!"

Steve raised the remote and paused the show there to inform my parents with a snort, "Yeah, I can tell you right now, that's definitely gonna go viral!"

"Do you think we should warn her?" Mom asked worriedly.

"She doesn't want us talking with her about it, Nita," Dad pointed out. "How many times has she already said that?"

"I know, but I'd hate for her to see it onli—oh, honey, we didn't see you standing there!"

My parents and my little brother turned on the couch to stare at me wide-eyed. Like a chicken had just walked in on them devouring a bucket of KFC.

Dad snatched the remote from Stevie and quickly hit the power off button.

The picture of the three men on TV disappeared, and Mom turned her attention to the laundry basket in my hands.

"Did you want to do a load of laundry?" she asked with an apologetic wince. "I just put one in for your little brother. But the washing machine should be free in an hour."

I blinked. Numbly.

Then I said to my brother. "Don't forget to come back on Saturday with your truck. The thrift store opens at 10 a.m."

"Honey, you're not really going to go through with that, are you?" Mom glanced at the huge Je T'aime Tourdin box that had been sitting in our living room since some international delivery service dropped it off while I was at work. "I mean, you didn't even open it, and you're just going to give all those clothes away to some thrift store?"

I loved my parents. And it wasn't their fault that they'd raised a too-trusting idiot for a daughter and a grown son with a shared apartment and truck who still came over every Monday to have Mommy take care of his laundry.

I knew that they were doing their best under the very weird circumstances. But I just couldn't tonight.

"I'll come back in an hour to put in my load," I muttered to Mom before returning to my room without a word.

However, I ended up falling asleep before the hour was done. That night, Mick showed up at our door with a smug soccer player who looked exactly like him to explain that Paris had all been a big misunderstanding. Of course, he hadn't lied to me. Mick truly was a power company electrician who loved me. And Andy, the soccer player, was just somebody who looked exactly like him.

But, of course, it was just a dream...

I woke up at five a.m. the next morning in the same bedroom I'd had all my life and a burning need to get to work early.

Anything to fill up this endless expanse of time.

Unfortunately, though, I was all out of laundry, having not put in a load since, like, a week before the trip my father refused to let me skip.

Which was how I came to find myself back in the living room at the crack of dawn, grumpily opening the Je T'aime Tourdin box with the sole intent of grabbing a top and bottom. Just one outfit to get me through until I washed my clothes that night.

But the sight of the box's contents stopped my heart.

There weren't just a few outfits for work but an entire wardrobe on a standing rack.

The bottoms were pretty much what I'd seen on the runway: fashionable trousers, ponte pants, and pencil skirts, but the mostly black offerings had been swapped out for winter shades I'd never tried before, like electric blues, quilted emeralds, and deep amethyst purples.

In my shopping life, bottoms had always been a sturdy purchase. I only bought standard colors that could match anything. But I could immediately tell that these eye-catching shades would pair well with any of the colorful tops hanging on the rack alongside them.

The blouses and shirts were even more vibrant—a colorful array of perennial trends like peplums, tie fronts, and scoop necks. They were all more than appropriate for work but could easily be dressed down for play, too.

I stared open-mouthed at the collection—all tailored to my measurements—and suddenly understood the true meaning of *couture*.

Even before I donned a frost pink jacquard top and paired it with a velvet plum skirt, I knew that I'd look like a million bucks in anything I wore out of this box of perfect-for-me clothes that Mick had handpicked himself.

And I wasn't wrong. A few minutes and one shower later, I found myself in front of my back-of-the-door full-length mirror, staring at a woman who was outwardly smart and capable with a happy personality.

Usually, I settled for wearing brightly colored underwear beneath my otherwise drab work clothes. But this outfit felt like a reflection of my true personality. The real me.

Was this how Mick had seen me? Even as he was using me all along?

I knew that if I told you everythin', you wouldn't understand that I was the exception to your new rule.

Mick's words from the Tourmaline argument whispered through my mind, breaking through the wall of numb I'd constructed around myself since returning early from Paris.

But then another voice invaded my mind.

"When you think about it, it was really quite brilliant. He shows up in Paris with this unknown woman and acts like he's completely in love with his holiday fling. The French press goes crazy. Meanwhile, he's showing the AS Paris Triomphe two things: One, he can fit in with their club's culture—he's not an antisocial psychopath as he sometimes comes off as here in England. And two: he can attract media and fan interest. With this holiday fling story, he was basically showing Paris Triomphe: Look, The Atomic Foot might be creeping up on thirty and heading into his sunset years, but he's a great player and a right interesting media personality who can put

bottoms in stadium seats. Definitely worth that massive payday he'll be receiving from the French club..."

That was as far as I had gotten in the clip of an English sports program in which three hosts were debating—but mostly praising —The Atomic Foot's ruthless business strategy for attracting a deal that would put him on the list of the top five most well-paid soccer players in the world.

But that was all I'd needed to hear—all I needed to *remember*.

I was a pawn, I reminded myself, turning away from my reflection. And "Mick" was a player in every sense of the word.

This outfit meant nothing. It was just a consolation prize for so naively falling in line with his ruthless plan.

I snatched up my phone from the charger and texted my brother.

10 am sharp on Saturday! Don't forget!

Then, I grabbed my keys and headed to work.

CHAPTER 21
Kayla

"Okay, two questions. One: Where did you get that top? Girl, it is *too cute*. And two: Why are you here so early?"

About an hour after my arrival at the Suns' sprawling front office on the top floor of a sleek complex overlooking the team's outdoor practice field, I looked up to find Suzie standing at my cubicle's entrance.

However, I didn't excitedly tell my bestie where I'd gotten the top, like I would have just a week ago—before I returned from Paris, a shell of my former self.

Instead, I answered, "I'm just working on the end-of-year report for your meeting with the owners."

"Thank you?" Suzie's reply came out as more of a question than a gratitude. "But you know that report's not due for another couple of weeks, right?"

"Yeah, I know that!" I snapped before I could stop myself. "But we don't always have to do things last-minute, do we? For once, let's do the practical thing and actually get ahead of the due date so it doesn't blow up in our faces!"

"Okay, why do I get a feeling that you suddenly deciding you just have to reconcile all our past year's numbers two weeks before they're due isn't just about you being the best payroll administrator on my team?"

Instead of snapping back at me, Suzie came farther into the office and set her large mom bag down on my desk. "You know, I'm here for you if you ever want to talk about what happened in Paris."

"Yes, I do know that, and I'm sorry for snapping." My burst of anger dissipated on a weary sigh. "But, no, I don't want to talk about it. I just want to do my work."

Ahead of time, if that's what it takes to fill up all my empty days.

Speaking of which, an idea suddenly occurred to me.

"Oh, hey, are you and Jay free this weekend?" I asked her. "I have to drop something off at the closest thrift store on Saturday morning, but after that, I was thinking the three of us could go to Lake Havasu."

"Lake Havasu? Like, in Arizona?" Suzie shook her head. "Why would you want to go there?"

"I dunno," I answered. "It just occurred to me while I was in Paris that I've never really been anywhere. And, hey, did you know Lake Havasu is where the old London Bridge is located now?"

Suzie furrowed her brow. "You mean, like the one from the song?"

"Actually, the one that was built to replace the one in the song— but close enough. And it's not in London anymore."

I swiveled around in my office chair to give her a breakdown of the whole story. "Basically, London was going to tear it down back in the late 60s, but some American investor was like, no, let me buy it, and I'll rebuild it in Lake Havasu. So, he did—then he died of a drug overdose less than 10 years later—because, you know, L.A. in the 70s. But the bridge is still there. Less than a six-hour drive away. Jay would probably love to see it."

"You want to take a grade-schooler who's usually all about his video games on the weekends to Arizona to show him a *bridge*?" Suzie asked with a skeptical look.

"Yeah! Why not?" I meant to sound enthusiastic, but my voice took on a weird, almost panicked note. "I mean, has he ever been to Arizona? Has he ever been anywhere but here in L.A., where he's always been every freaking day of his life?"

Suzie regarded me for a couple of beats, then appeared to decide to say, "Actually, we do have plans. Maybe next month? I know Jay's off one of those February Mondays—oh, and hey, I saw your mom last week, and she was saying something about maybe the three of us getting together on Sunday after the playoff game to discuss the new Clara Quinn book. I was planning on downloading it on audio to get ready for it. So, I'm not sure either of us would have been free to spend a weekend in Arizona anyway."

"Zephyr was the one who kidnapped her," I answered dully.

"What?" Suzie's expression was beyond confused.

My voice took on a bitter tone as I spoiled the story for her without an ounce of remorse. "Zephyr had his own bride kidnapped to save her from their enemies. And despite everything they'd been through, he wiped her memories. So now Aziza is stuck back in the human dimension with no idea that she was slated to become Queen of the Wind Fae. And Zephyr said he did it for her own good, but that was as far as I got before I threw my e-reader across the room!"

I expelled a growl of rage at the memory of not being able to take solace in the latest Fae of the Realm book after I returned from Paris. "Forget Clara Quinn!"

"Forget Clara Quinn?" Suzie repeated. "Your favorite writer of all time? The one you told me I had to start reading if I wanted us to stay friends?"

"Yeah, forget her!" I insisted. "She's a jerk who glorifies jerks. I mean, Zephyr thought he knew *so* much better than Aziza? He just had to go decide her whole life for her? Move her around like a pawn in his Fae Realm war games? No! No! I couldn't keep reading after he did that!"

Several beats. Then with a careful tone, Suzie asked, "Are you *sure* you don't want to talk about Par—"

"No! I don't want to talk about Paris!" I practically shouted to the heavens before she could finish asking me that question yet again.

"Girl, I'm just trying to—"

"I know! I know!" I rubbed two hands over my tired face and found myself having to apologize again for the second time in what couldn't have even been two minutes of conversation. "I'm sorry, Suze. Just give me a few more days. I'm sure I'll be over this by the end of the month."

Suzie's expression told me she clearly didn't believe me, but she hefted her purse back on her arm anyway.

"Well, you know I'm always here for you, girl, *whenever* you need me," she said, preparing to leave me to my way-earlier-than-required numbers checking.

"I know, and I'm grateful," I answered, turning back to my laptop to resume my miserable number crunch.

Until it occurred to me to ask. "Wait, why are *you* here so early?"

"Oh, ah..." Suzie paused on her way out of my cubicle. "After approving your PTO over the payday, I decided to invest in early drop-off at Jay's school for the month of January to give myself some extra time in the morning, you know, just in case I needed it. But it's been so nice having another hour to get situated before work. I'm kind of thinking of opting for early drop-off in February too."

I narrowed my eyes. "So, you've been coming in this early since last week?"

"Yeah, I know it's a lot of money just to give myself prep time...." she began to say, obviously mistaking the reason I was giving her a weird look.

"No, I'm wondering why it took you so long to return my text about Dwayne being cut from the team if you were here at the office way before eight a.m."

"Oh, I..." Suzie fiddled with the strap of her huge purse and glanced to the side. "Guess I got busy. And, like I said, you didn't need to be worrying about Dwayne anyway."

Her vague answer made me narrow my eyes even more.

She was lying! To *me*. Her best friend. I might not have been able to intuit that a week ago, but now I sensed it clear as day.

I'd been so caught up, replaying over and over again what happened with Andy-slash-Mick, that it hadn't occurred to me to re-question what had happened in the hours leading up to Dwayne's big reveal.

The many hours it had taken Suzie to get back to me.

"I'd still be on the Suns' roster if it wasn't for you!"

Dwayne's strange casting of blame in front of the Benton Budget popped back into my head...along with a new suspicion.

"Did you have something to do with Dwayne getting cut from the team? Is that why you didn't bring it up when I told you about my fling with the Brit while I was in Paris?"

Suzie answered this question much faster than the other one. "No, I didn't get Dwayne fired! Not me."

Yep, the old Kayla, who trusted without question, had definitely left the building. Suzie's "not me" made me ask, "Then *who*?"

"Who?" Suzie repeated, obviously stalling for time. She was probably hoping I'd sense her discomfort and back off the subject.

That was what old Kayla would have done.

But old Kayla was gone.

New Kayla looked her best friend dead in the eye and repeated, "*Who*?"

Suzie looked to both sides like she was trying to come up with a cover story.

But then she caved with a, "Look, Kayla, you were planning to spend a week of PTO sulking over Dwayne in your room. Of course, your parents and I were worried about what would happen when the team came back from their break."

I held up my hands. "Wait, so you and my parents got together like some kind of "we're worried about Kayla" cabal and just decided to get Dwayne cut from the team?"

"You're making it sound like this was a huge conspiracy." Suzie put up her hands defensively. "Frankly, Dwayne isn't that good of a player. He barely survived the post-season cut. And you know how much the coaching team respects your dad's opinion. It was easy for him to drop a bug in their ear."

"Easy?" I repeated. Anger gathered in my chest like a new storm. "Easy to manipulate my life while I was away. That's what you really mean! You didn't think I could handle Dwayne."

"It wasn't manipulation," Suzie countered with an insistent shake of her head. "You're my best friend and my best payroll administrator. I couldn't have you putting in your two weeks' notice, like, a day or two after the Suns came back from break."

Run! Run like the coward you are. Because you're weak—incapable of fighting for anything.

"You think I'm a coward?" I asked Suzie with Andy Atwater's words echoing in my mind. "You all truly believed that I would quit, just so I didn't have to cut Dwayne a paycheck?"

Suzie looked to the side. "Well, you dropped out of college, like, a week after transferring to SCU because your counselor said you needed to pick a major."

"Because I wasn't sure what I wanted, and I didn't need to waste a bunch of money finding myself."

"And you gave up your condo search last year, even after you saved up enough for a down payment."

"Because the L.A. market is *insane,* and I was fine at home!"

"Okay, well, then call it an abundance of caution." Suzie dipped her head and threw me a sympathetic look. "We just wanted to make sure you felt comfortable here when you returned. You know, *safe.*"

Safe...

That's the real reason you stayed with this wanker for as long as you did, innit? Because he was safe. Cos you thought he was some nice Missouri boy, and you were afraid of datin' someone you felt somethin' real for. Someone like me!

Suzie's excuse for why she and my parents had worked behind the scenes to get Dwayne fired put my entire life in relief.

Suddenly, all my reasons for living the way I did sounded less like good sense and more like fear. New questions piled up in my head.

Had I dropped out of SCU because I was afraid to follow my interests and see where a bachelor's degree would lead me?

Had I chosen to work for the Suns—or settled for this position because the L.A. job market was a big and scary place?

Just like the housing market that had me still sleeping in the same bedroom where I'd grown up? The same bedroom I'd slept in every single week of my adult life?

Until Mick.

With Mick, I'd taken chances. All the chances. With Mick, I'd been brave.

My heart sped up, remembering the look on his face when he predicted I'd run away as opposed to staying to fight. *For us.*

But leaving had been the right thing to do... hadn't it?

The sound of voices in the distance interrupted my sudden questioning of every *safe* decision I'd ever made in my life. Safe decisions that definitely did not match the outfit I was currently wearing—the outfit the man I'd known as Mick had picked out for me.

"Hey, you know what, on second thought, getting a head start on the end-of-year report is a great idea," Suzie said, glancing over her shoulder at the other early arrivals. "Want to use the conference room, so you can really spread out?"

"Sure," I answered, trying to match her bright work tone. But my voice sounded weak, even to my own ears.

Suzie rushed away, and I thought about texting my parents to get their side of the story.

But why? Suzie had explained their reasoning loud and clear.

I always played it safe, so they'd decided to play it safe for me on my behalf.

Maybe I could have blamed them, but Mick's final words to me were ringing too loud in my ears.

As I put together the report in the conference room, thoughts of what Mick had said about why I really wouldn't stay and hear him out swirled in my head.

Confusing me. Hindering my concentration.

And then, I caught my reflection in the glass conference room windows...

I miss her. I miss the woman I was when I was with him.

The thoughts suddenly broke through on a cresting wave of sadness.

And I miss Mick even more.

Even though I knew the stranger I met on the way to Paris was really a soccer player named Andy, and the character of "Mick" was completely made up, it didn't change one fact.

I'd fallen in love with him. And that love hadn't immediately turned to bitter ashes like it had with Dwayne.

Underneath the anger. Underneath the sadness, it continued to burn.

Along with a terrible feeling that I'd lost something magical when I walked out of the Tourmaline's lobby. Something I'd never get back. No matter how much time passed.

"Hey, I got us Roscoe's for lunch!" a chipper voice announced behind me.

I turned around to find Suzie in the doorway of the conference room, holding up a takeout bag from the Inglewood location of the iconic chicken and waffles restaurant in her hand.

Wait, it was already time to eat lunch? How long had I been spinning over Mick? Wondering if I got it all wrong?

"Hey! I don't have to watch Scuzz on TV *every day*," Suzie said, mistaking the reason for my stunned expression.

I looked at Suzie.

Then looked into the depths of my soul.

Then I said, "I think I do want to talk about Paris. Actually, I really need to talk to someone about what happened with Mick."

CHAPTER 22

Kayla

BY THE TIME I WAS DONE WITH THE WHOLE STORY, there were only bones, crumbs, and dots of syrup left in our individual takeout containers, and Suzie was all empathetic nods.

"You're beating yourself up for falling too fast, but I get it, girl, I do."

She let out a self-deprecating laugh. "Actually, letting myself fall too far, too fast, with the wrong person was how I got Jay. I don't regret him for a second, but...."

She trailed off and got quiet before admitting. "Tag called me a little over a week ago. The Suns management isn't going to announce it until after The Big Game in February, but they're planning to sign him on as the team's new quarterback. And he wants to revisit the complete-revocation-of-parental-rights custody agreement he signed before Jay was born."

"Oh, my gosh, Suzie! Forget my stuff!" I reached across the table to grab onto my best friend's hand. "That's crazy! What are you going to do?"

Suzie didn't talk much about Noah "Tag" Taggart, the now famous quarterback that she'd once dated when they both attended Southern California University. But from what I could tell, they'd burned bright and hot—all the way until their spectacular breakup, right after she told him she was pregnant with Jay.

Which was why she'd established a rule against dating football players, even before my mom recommended her for a job working for the Suns. But while I was in Paris, apparently, the team's owners had decided that her son's father would be the best replacement for our low-performing quarterback. And now Tag, who'd earned worldwide fame and millions of dollars throughout his playing career without acknowledging his son, was asking to be let back into Jay's life.

Which meant she was going to have to make some hard decisions on behalf of her ten-year-old son, who'd only ever known Suzie as a parent.

"Even after nearly two weeks of spinning on it, I have no idea," Suzie admitted, answering my question about her next steps with a broken laugh. "I think that's the real reason I was suddenly so hot to talk to your dad about getting Dwayne cut from the team. I've got Jay to think about, and I can't just up and leave this cushy job —especially if there's a custody fight in my future. But I didn't see any reason for both of us to suffer when spring rolls around."

Suzie's eyes shadowed. "Just be grateful you found out what kind of guy this soccer player really was before you made something permanent with him."

She was right. Yet, my heart panged remembering what Andy/Mick had said about wanting to be a father, the opposite of the one he'd had growing up.

As ruthless as he'd proven himself to be since that conversation, I still couldn't see him agreeing to give up his parental rights like Tag had.

"I love you...I love you... I love you."

The words that the man I knew as Mick chanted in my ear the last time we were together echoed across my memory.

Why had he said that? I wondered bitterly—not for the first time.

His claiming to love me and agreeing to stay an additional 3 days to keep me company was the only thing that didn't make sense. And he'd seemed truly sincere about the idea of becoming a father.

Would he eventually live out that dream with the "right" woman? Maybe a model or someone else as famous and rich as him?

The vibration of my phone on the table interrupted the unsettling thought of him moving on as if Paris never happened.

It was a call from a number I didn't recognize.

"Probably Dwayne again," I told Suzie, sending the call straight to voicemail.

It was a California 2-1-3 area code this time—not the Missouri 3-1-4 numbers he'd used in the lead-up to Paris—but I wouldn't put it past him to figure out yet another way to cloak his number.

"Do you need to get a restraining order?" Suzie asked.

"I don't think so." I set the phone back on the table, this time face down so that I could ignore the inevitable follow-up texts that always trailed behind one of Dwayne's calls. "I made it clear we have no future, and I think he's too broke and jobless to pull off another in-person show-up. That last-minute ticket to Paris was not in his best interest."

"No, it was not," Suzie agreed with a completely unsympathetic click of her tongue. "Though you still might want to think about changing your—"

"'Scuse me, 'scuse me. This thing on?" A voice suddenly boomed out over the front office's P.A. system.

I froze because the voice's accent was unmistakably English.

But no, it couldn't be...

"This is Mick Atwater," the voice assured me before I could finish that thought.

"This is Mick Atwater," the voice announced before she could finish. "Andy Atwater if real Football's yer thing. Anyway, could you help a bloke out? I'm completely lost in this Byzantine cubicle farm, and I'm trying to find Kayla Edwards. I believe she works here?"

I rose to my feet. Oh. My. God. Mick...I mean, *Andy* was here. In L.A. At my office!

"Haven't you embarrassed that poor woman enough?" a co-worker demanded on the overhead, close enough to be picked up by the P.A. system's microphone.

"Yeah," another voice agreed. "Kayla's a good person. She didn't deserve what you did to her in Paris. Especially after Dwayne."

I didn't know whether to be embarrassed or grateful to my co-workers, who were apparently taking it upon themselves to tell off the star soccer player who broke my heart.

Either way, I started to rush toward the door to cut this conversation short.

But Suzie grabbed my shoulder in one hand and the conference room phone in the other. "No, I'll call security. You said your piece in Paris. You don't need to give him the satisfaction of another fight."

Mick's voice sounded on the overhead speaker before I could answer.

"I'm going to have to disagree with ya there, mate," he said to the unseen co-worker. "She's not a *good* woman. She is the *best* woman I've ever known."

"Then why did you hurt her like that?" one of the voices demanded.

And another one added, "Why are you even here?"

Suzie was right about me not rushing out there to take part in another scene. But I found myself making a motion for her to put down the conference room's handset because I wanted to hear the answer to those questions myself.

"Good questions," Mick answered. "You, like Kayla and plenty of those smug media bastards, probably think I misled her for some deal and a little bit of holiday fun. And ya know what? I did do that? At first, I saw it as an opportunity within an opportunity, if ya know what mean. Plan was to get in, get out, then move right on. But here's where the story gets complicated..."

The glassed-in offices and conference rooms were located on the opposite side of the sprawling cubicle farm than the reception desk where the P.A. system lived. So, I couldn't see Mick.

But by this point, several more of the hundred-plus people who worked in the Suns front office's cubicle farm popped up like gophers from their desks to listen to Mick's side of the story.

Even Suzie was mesmerized. She not only put down the phone, but she came over to stand with me beneath the conference's intercom system to hear what he said next.

"I couldn't move on cos Kayla is wonderful, addictive, the most easy person I've ever met to be around—not to mention incredibly beautiful, innit she?" Mick continued. "And, when you meet somebody who's wonderful like that, someone who gets you—even the bad parts, what are you gonna do when she tells you she's gone off professional athletes because of her wanker ex? Tell Miss Most Wonderful Woman Ya Ever Met, 'Ah, well,' that's a'right, then, maybe next lifetime'?"

Mick made a scoffing sound in response to his own question. "Nah, I couldn't bring meself to do that. So, I ended up doin' somethin' way worse. I misled her. I decided to do whatever it took to keep her, including outright lie."

Several boos went up from a few of the people in the office as if the opposing team had just fouled one of our players.

"That's right. Boo! Boo!!! Fuck me all the way back to England!" Mick replied, in seeming full agreement with his naysayers. "Truth is, I deserved that slap and a good kick in the goolies besides. But what ya don't understand, what I don't think she understood, the guy I was pretendin' to be so I could remain in her orbit—not just her knickers—*that* was the guy I *wanted* to be—not whatever Frankenstein of branding and ego Andrew Michael Atwater was supposed to be."

His voice grew softer. "More than anythin', I wanted to be somebody who could make a woman like Kayla look at him like he was worthy of her, like he deserved a role in her universe. So yeah, I lied and all that. But not about the important stuff, not about how totally, completely, impractically in love I was with her from day one. And not about how much I love her *still?*"

He loved me? Like, truly loved me? Still? Even after the deal had gone through and he'd gotten everything he wanted.

I exchanged a stunned look with Suzie, not sure how to process all of this.

"So, why am I here, one of you asked?"

Mick came back to the earlier question. "Short answer. Sleep Deprivation. I had it in my mind after that slap that I was going to leave Kayla be because the truth is she deserves better than me. But that was a week ago, on a full night of sleep, and I haven't really slept since I left Paris without the woman I love, have I? That's another thing about Kayla. When I was with her, I'll tell you this, mate, I slept like a baby. Now that she's gone... no sleep. Just tossing and turning, replaying how it all fell apart. Wondering if there was anything I could've said or done to make it go different."

"So, you decided to humiliate her again at her office?" one of the people standing close enough to get picked up on the system's microphone asked, her voice full of outrage on my behalf.

"I tell you, it wasn't even a decision." Mick's voice sounded weary. "One moment, an assistant coach is telling us we've got two mandatory rest days after our last match. And the next thing I knew, I was at Heathrow, booking meself a flight to Los Angeles, taking a taxi from the airport directly here cos all I really know 'bout Kayla's life in L.A. is that she has great parents, she has a best friend who's also her boss, and she works in the payroll area for the Suns. To be frank, I'm not even sure if I'm in the right office. This stadium office is loads bigger than the one in London or Paris. You Americans really like to build your spaces big. That's not just a rumor."

Another chuff, then his voice grew serious again. "But I had to try. If you're listening, Kayla, I need to give you the honest truth. I had no business calling you a coward in that lobby. It was me who played scared ball with you. Hiding my true intentions and motives when you told me from the start—I mean, from our very first conversation how important it was to be honest with you."

I'd been successfully holding back my tears since Paris, but I lost the battle in an instant. My eyes filled with them as I listened to Mick talk directly to me through the overhead.

"So, here's me being honest. I honestly love you, Kayla. I honestly want you to quit your job without notice and come back to London with me right now."

A few of my co-workers booed again.

But Mick's voice was unrepentant. "I'm just being honest here, mates—like I said. Like I promise to be from now on. *Kayla,*I got a burnin' need to marry you and start a family—preferably two girls cos if I learned anythin' from this experience, it's that boys are stupid. I want us to pick a place in Paris together—somewhere we can look down at the city glowing at night when we move there in August. Whatever dream you have for your life, love, I want to make it come true. Because you are the dream I was too scared to have before we met, and now, all I want to do is spend the rest of my living this dream with you. Don't say no, Kayla. Please, one last time. Don't say no."

I could barely breathe, my heart was beating so fast.

I looked at Suzie, who stared back at me wide-eyed.

"What are you thinking right now?" she said in that careful way she always used when she was withholding her opinion to see what I said first.

"That he's crazy," I answered.

But then I added, "That I must be crazy, too, because I'm so happy right now. And I really want to go to him, even if it is in no way safe."

"Good, we're on the same page." Suzie let out a relieved breath. "Girl, that was so ridiculously romantic—I will write your letter of resignation my own damn self. You better go to that man!"

I ripped open the conference room's glass door and ran down the main row of the cubicle farm until I found Mick leaned over the microphone at reception, his neck craning around.

"Kayla? Kayla? I'm beginnin' to suspect she's out to lunch, and none of you lot got 'round to tellin' me that before I made a fool of meself. If so, let me tell ya, that's completely outta bounds—oh, there ya are, love!"

Mick's face crumpled at the sight of me. Then completely lit up. "Is that a yes, then?"

Was that a yes?

My answer to that question came in the form of me closing the space between us and throwing myself into his arms without any warning.

But Mick didn't need any warning. He caught me easily and kissed me like a man long deprived of oxygen, holding onto me like he would never let me go. And at that moment, I knew one thing for sure....

No more playing it safe.

My one-night stand with the stranger on the plane had just been extended to a lifetime.

OH MY GOSH, THANK YOU SO MUCH FOR READING KAYLA IN PARIS!

Do you want one more scene with this crazy-but-delightful couple after they move to Paris? Then click here to sign up for my newsletter and the KAYLA IN PARIS Bonus Epilogue, which will drop on February 4th!

You'll also be able to find out more about the next books in the Ruthless Magnates series: **Sunny in Vegas** and **Prudence in New Orleans** (featuring Max Benton).

Meanwhile, if you loved Mick's and Kayla's story please make sure to leave a review of wherever you got this book!

Special Thanks to My Ruthless Patreons!

Become a Ruthless Patreon!

<u>Ruthless Mega</u>
Laila Henriksen
Janet
Shante Simpkins
Akisha
Monique Freeman
Lica N.
Quin Nesselhauf
Nicole
Beatrice
Tammy
Cynthea Carbon
MJ Evans
Vernecia McCall
Monique A.
Shaneka Nichols
Anita Allen
Colleen

Julienne

Ruthless Super-Duper
Carla Truss
Ashley McSevney
lisa
Georgette Connell
CrystaM0
Hannah Kirstin
tameka teal
Nicol
Susan Hall Comrie
MonaGirl Lewis
Leslie Tucker
Fredericka C Hudson
Sharon Keyes
Josephine Thompson
Sandra Wynn
Nubooti
Patricia Cardinal
Vanessa F A
Sonya Barry
Mylene Williams

Ruthless Super
Fanny Mateo
Mjl
WakeUpMakeUp Slay
Shalenna Lucas
Bojana Pavicevic
Zay
Deb Derrepente
Lady Hawke
Nikki

Grace

Vickie

Simp

Dr. CC

Colleen OKeeffe

Danette

Kim

Ray

Danyelle

RONI WAWA

Amy

Denise Dabney

Nadia Penn

Sasha Steele

Kazi Ahmed

Karen

L Burden

Tiffany P

Shawnie

Denise Hughes

Nilise

SokkasGirl

Nina Sandra

Terri Thao

Natalie D. Eckman

Nita Field

Deja

JYELVERTON

Leah

Naturalbrainiac

K. Brown

Sandi Hospedales

Hin Lee

Kimmey

Daeterria McLucas
Beverley Jackson
Darcy Leone
Chinyere Offor
OOW
Deanna Rivera
Billie Henry
Dana R
Evelyn Green
Manoucheka Chery
Tiffany Burns
Biaunca Albury
Lashan Delancy
Ayalibis Dowell
Christine Roth
Andrea
Jenetha Williams
Nicole H
Lyndetta Timmons
Latricia Warren
Clustelle Nielle Charles
Alice Rutland
Tiffany Mays
Petra Malusclava
Brenda
Hridhi Islam
Sonya Napier
Shiva
Dana Sandoval
Marianne K.
Tanecia Appling
Sheryl Wilder
Tasha
Jaleda Wyatt

Ruthless Fan

Lew

Shon Brown

Monica Overtone

Rochelle Younger

Yolanda Sullivan

karezone

Shanice

fayola alibey

J Gordon

Kellee Wilhite

Rebecka Lancelot

Nzinga West

GILLIAN SUTHERLIN

Paula Silas-Guy

Jennifer Lindsey

Lisa

Stephanie Hall

Jackie

Kenya Wright

nanc evans

Ayesha Cruickshank

Sharon McDowall

Nene

Toni

stacey kindles

Anissa M Jones

Courtney McFadden

Free

Andrea

Ashleigh Dixon

Shronda C.

T. Williams

Nakia Wooley

Keri Stevens
Kia

Ruthless Readers
Farah Ware
Lani3a
Laura Royals
Forever Trill
Gina Sturgis
Mikki
Rina Thompson
romance_reader
Sercee
Kandi Facison
Marielle Sobowale
Lani D. Lester
Shannon Harris
Marina Benitez
Tracy Williams
Mo
Nicole Pack
Renee
Shelby Edwards
Nicole Woodard
Danielle
cmdennis
Haniel Udubra
Tamika Jones
Lindsey Buch
Jessica Madsen
Sherri Tillman
Stacie Ervin
Vanita
Angela Burns

RL McGruder

Stephanie Palacio

Teneatha Jackson

Fathom Watson

Lori

Mechelle Bagot

Autumn Park

Liz Lincoln

Melody

Nadine Smith

Laura Ross

Karen palmer

Marian Cork Barbary

Kay Lamb

Oratile Ntimane

Yolanda Clemons

Jackie Karnley

Anna.Vassell

Robin Glenn

Natalie sang

Tangela McGee

Rukiya Caldwell

Henrietta Appiah

Devorah Proctor

Z Mol

Wynette Houston

Rashida Harrison

Twiza Kathleen

JLA

Ebony

Anastacia Isaacs

Kier101 0

Eliza F

Renee cox

Eli Kingkade
Dionte Murph
Angela Ramey
Felisha Workman
Michelle Smith
Angela
Nikki E
Tea.S
Tiffany Hereford
Chance
Ebony Harvey
Deirdre Pierce
Machelle Bryson
Gaelle Berclaz
Keva Wilson
Angela Ball
Eboni
Teresa Saez
Janel Chapman
Alexa Abdelatey
Diana
Tiffanie Oakley
Barbara
Annette Wynne
Mary
Bernadette Mason
Sylvia Thomas
Janice Hipps
KB
Jakea Leakes
Lisema Sinord
Freja T
Shawn
Elle

Tonya Collins
Toni
Andrea Mclin
Caroline Jones
Deborah Smith
Shawnte Reasor
Paula Thompson
Tykeisha Rice
AsiaRenee
Cecile
April Marro
Amy Mathews
Antoinette Green
Ramona L Green
latosha johnson
material.gworl
Sonya Som
BF Smith
Toi
Kamico Seals
Nicole Kohlmeier
Ama misa
Nina Moore
Claudia Ferreira
Kisha Caldwell
Jacqueline Britt
Andrea Gregory
Val Zaharia
Lethia M Grimes
Free Peay
Shalaia Walters
Kimberly Ellis
Jeanine Hawkins
Simone Howard

Julie

Judith

Cynthia Mckissick

Shayna Hayes

Lynn Leary

Judy

Neah White

WC Ford

Linda Browne

Monique Biggett-Johnson

Deidre Clayburn

Babette Cooper

Terri Robinson

Earline Stephen

Kali Murray

Johari Crews

Lynnette M

Erica Severan

Adrienne Jones

Christian Hibbard

Ava Nichol

Anita Burge

Phyllis Harrington

Roxanne

Heather Goltz

OAA

Alexis M.

LaTarsha Morrison

Lilith Darville

Become a Ruthless Patreon

Also by Theodora Taylor

About the Author

Theodora Taylor writes hot books with heart. When not reading, writing, or reviewing, she enjoys spending time with her amazing family, going on date nights with her wonderful husband, and attending parties thrown by others. She LOVES to hear from readers. So....

Join TT's Patreon
https://www.patreon.com/theodorataylor

Follow TT on TikTok
https://www.tiktok.com/@theodorataylor100

Follow TT on Instagram
https://www.instagram.com/taylor.theodora/

Sign for up for TT's Newsletter
http://theodorataylor.com/sign-up/

Join the Ruthless Romance Readers on Facebook
https://www.facebook.com/ruthlessromancereaders

Printed in Great Britain
by Amazon